# Fig.

THIS BOOK IS THE PROPERTY OF
POCKLINGTON SCHOOL

| | NAME | Date of Issue | Initials |
|---|---|---|---|
| 1 | Don Wilson | 4/1/96 | DA |
| 2 | Phill Welsh | 30/1/6 | |
| 3 | Emma Clark | 11/11/98 | HM |
| 4 | Rupert Briggs | 30/10/99 | NH |
| 5 | | | |

*Other BYKER GROVE titles from BBC Books:*

BYKER GROVE
HEARTBREAK FOR DONNA
ODD ONE OUT
TURNING ON, TUNING IN
GREEN FOR DANGER
LOVE WITHOUT HOPE

# Fighting Back

*Wally K Daly*

BBC Books

For Adéle Rose, who wrote
the six television episodes on
which this novelisation is based.

BYKER GROVE is a
Zenith North Production

Published by BBC Books,
a division of BBC Enterprises Limited,
Woodlands, 80 Wood Lane, London W12 0TT

First published 1991
© Wally K. Daly 1991
ISBN 0 563 36271 5

Set in Baskerville by Redwood Press Limited, Melksham, Wiltshire
Printed and bound in Great Britain by Clays Ltd, St Ives plc.
Cover printed by Clays Ltd, St Ives plc.

# CHAPTER ONE

Speedy's life had been changed forever, by the tops of three cereal packets, and a six-word jingle he had written while he was eating a bowl of the very same cereal. Having come to terms with the fact that Charlie, the beautiful Charlie who he'd fallen so desperately in love with, was never going to consider him as any more than 'Just Speedy', he knew he had to use every possible trick at his disposal to get her out of his mind, and keep her out for good.

It wasn't easy.

He found that writing songs didn't help. No matter how hard he tried to avoid it, all the lyrics he wrote seemed to end up being about her, and were universally depressing and miserable.

So he bravely told his new friend Danny round at Dimmoro's café, that he wanted to put their song-writing career on the back burner for a while. Danny accepted happily enough as his new job, helping out the local milkman, was proving more taxing than he'd anticipated.

Speedy, in his search of a suitable occupation to drive out the constant pictures of Charlie that invaded his mind, finally found one that worked really well. Reading. He'd never been a great fan of reading before, being honest, always preferring physical activity – football, cricket or whatever – to what he considered to be a fairly boring school-based occupation. Of course he'd read what he had to for school work purposes, but had never got around to reading for pleasure. Until now that was, and it was an eye opener. He found that if he read out loud in his head, whether it was books, magazines, newspapers or whatever, the pictures of Charlie had no room to arrive in his brain and haunt him, and for minutes at a time he could stop himself thinking about her altogether. Wonderful.

Lou, foster mother to the ill-assorted bunch of waifs and strays that were always gathered under her roof on a long term basis at the initiative of the local social services, was initially pleased with the change she saw happening in Speedy.

She had of course been aware that he was going through an emotional bad patch, and had been all ready to pick up the pieces when the time was right. So she was pleased when it turned out there were no pieces to pick up. But soon it had gone to an extreme, and Speedy, even when at the table, would have his face buried in a book or paper and more often than not let the cooked breakfast she had made, go cold on the plate in front of him. Finally Lou had to take the extreme step of banning books and newspapers from the table.

This didn't stop Speedy reading of course. Now he'd found what worked he was going to stick at it until Charlie had gone from his thoughts for good. When it came to additional reading, everything on the table became fair game. From the back of the sauce bottle to the mustard pot, he could soon say word for word what was written on any item.

Then one morning a new cereal packet arrived. To get the product moving the company who made it was having a competition, and the rules were on the back of the box: SEND 3 CARTON TOPS AND A SIX-WORD SLOGAN, AND A BRAND NEW 18-GEAR RACING BIKE COULD BE YOURS. Between pouring his coffee and drinking it, Speedy had the words of a slogan written out; written so quickly in fact that later on he couldn't even remember what the words were, only knowing they were really good. Then, having snaffled the tops off the three packets of cereal he found in the pantry, Speedy got an envelope and stamp from the bureau, and on the way to school, posted tops, slogan, and his name and address off to the competition headquarters.

He then immediately forgot about it, and went back to reading books by the dozen.

He forgot about it, that is, until the knock came at the front door one month later, and the post van delivered a large parcel addressed to him, all wrapped in brown paper. There was no disguising it, it was a bicycle. He had won the competition, and, for the price of three cereal tops and a six-word slogan, Speedy's life was changed forever.

Speedy thought his thoughts as he strained to get to the top of the endless hill he was cycling up on his new bike, as he seemed to have been doing for hours. He ached in every muscle and fibre of his being from the balls of his feet to the white knuckles of his hands clutching the handlebars that he pulled up as his exhausted feet pushed down, driving him and his bicycle ever onwards and upwards. His calves felt as though they could snap at any second with the pressure he was putting on them to keep him and the bike moving, and there was no more gears at his disposal to make the going any easier. He saw the brow of the hill was in striking distance now and he counted out twenty downward pushes with each leg using the last vestige of his strength, and the final number, twenty, had him sweeping to the top of the hill, breasting it, and heading down the other side.

He could see for miles, but didn't know where he was. The country below had a strange air about it, but he quickly forgot the niggling worry as he started to gather speed and the sheer exhilaration of free-wheeling started to take over.

Now he was moving at ever increasing speed. The machine oiled and honed and tuned to perfection was humming silently along like a two-wheeled Rolls Royce. He realised that soon he would have to brake gently to ease his downward flight, but put it off for as long as he dared, just thrilling to the immense speed he was managing. He put the moment off, and put it off, but finally he could put it off no more, and applied the brakes gently.

Nothing happened.

More pressure. Still nothing. Then he jammed them full on. The bicycle simply increased its speed. He was hurtling down like a bullet. He could hear a strange sound like stones flinging up from the whirling wheels and pinging as if they were hitting glass, but the sound was lost in his panic as the reality of the situation hit home. The road below flattened and then quickly curved away to the right, but there was no way he could manage to take the curve at that speed.

He was going to hit the pavement!

And then he hit it with a sickening wheel-buckling thud; and he was off the bike and flying, his hands stretched out in front of him as if to ward off the tree that was directly in his flight path, but it was no good, it didn't move.

He was going to hit the tree head on!

He hit it and all went black.

The noise was intruding more clearly now. The ping of stone against glass.

Speedy flicked his eyes open. And was amazed to discover he was lying in his bed at the Gallaghers' completely undamaged, the dawn, a faint light behind the half open curtains at the window. Speedy sat up and looked at the clock, seven, and then lay back down again, and smiled at the thought that struck him. He spoke it out loud.

'I got the woman who gave me nightmares out of me head; and now me bloomin' bike is taking over.'

But his thoughts were interrupted abruptly as the noise came again. It *was* a pebble landing on the window.

He got out of bed and crossed to look downward through the gap in the curtain, and there was Winston all ready to sling another stone.

Speedy flung the window open and called:

'Haway, man, are you mad or what?'

Winston was obviously pleased to see him up and about.

'Upsadaisy, rise and shine.'

And then Speedy remembered what it was all about. There was to be a cycle race, and as the owner of the best bike in Byker Grove he was the one who was going to be doing the racing. Winston, un-asked, had declared himself Speedy's trainer.

There was only one answer, thought Speedy. Rudeness.

'Bog off.'

'You want to be at the peak of your physical perfection, don't you?'

'Not at seven in the morning, I don't.' But Speedy knew Winston. The one thing that was for sure was that he would go on standing there and nagging on till he gave in. So finally he admitted defeat.

'Hang on, Winston. Be down in a minute.'

'Good on ya, man! And don't forget your bike!'

A little while later in the kitchen at the Dobson house, Nicola fought an unequal battle against the combined noises of Jemma and Angel, who had been staying overnight, plus the toast-making of grandmother Mary, as she tried to get the homework that should have been completed the night before finished. It wasn't proving easy. The toaster's thermostat was obviously on the blink and every piece that Mary took out needed to have occasional burnt bits scraped off them into the sink; while Jemma was reading out loud from the problem page of a magazine, with Angel looking over her shoulder, adding in the appropriate laments.

'I'm in love with this lad, they call him Craig . . . *Aaah.*'

'*Aaaah.*'

They both giggled joyfully.

'But last week I found out he was two-timing me.' Angel was instantly alert for more discovery about the strange world of juvenile courtship.

'What's that mean?'

And Jemma was of course both suitably knowledgeable and able to administer a put-down in passing.

'Going with two girls at once, thicko.'

She was about to carry on reading, but Nicola got her comment in first.

'How can I concentrate with you two squawking like demented parrots?'

Jemma had no sympathy at all.

'Serves you right. Should have done your homework last night.' And having spoken a truth that Nicola could not deny, was immediately back reading out loud again.

'I can't stop thinking about him and he's broken my heart . . . *Aaaah!*'

'*Aaaah!*'

Mary paused mid scrape of the last piece of toast and directed her remark at Nicola.

'Speaking of broken hearts, how's your friend Charlie?'

Nicola decided to give up the struggle with her work and packed her books away as she spoke.

'I reckon she's getting over it.'

'Poor lad. I do hope he gets better.'

9

'Yeah. Poor old Robert. Dead sad.'

Jemma had stopped reading and couldn't resist throwing in her thought.

'Dead soppy, you mean.'

Nicola was appalled at her callousness.

'He couldn't walk, Jemma!'

Jemma wasn't impressed.

'Girls get soppy over lads even when they can't walk.'

Angel's single 'Yuck' indicated her agreement.

Mary brought the freshly scraped toast to the table, speaking to Jemma as she did so.

'So you're not going to fall in love, are you not, miss?'

Jemma was adamant in her rejection of the thought.

'No way. But they can fall in love with us if they like, can't they, Angel?'

'Yeah!'

As Mary put the toast down Jemma yanked Angel up.

'Come on, Angel. I want to get there early. Ricky Morgan's doing bowling practice.'

Nicola was perplexed at the instant change of gear.

'I thought you weren't interested in lads?'

'I only want to laugh at him. He's pathetic.'

As they both grabbed one last a piece of toast and headed for the door Angel remembered her manners.

'Thank you for having us, Mrs O'Malley.'

Considering how often Angel stayed these days Mary was momentarily thrown as to what she could possibly mean, but then she had it.

'It's a pleasure, pet. Any time.'

And as Nicola joined them and all three headed for the hall, she called to no one in particular.

'Call Debbie down, would you, she's going to be late.'

It was Jemma who popped her head back into the room and gave the answer. 'She's gone out.'

Mary was suitably surprised.

'At this time – where to?'

'Dunno.' Then Jemma giggled at the thought.

'Bet she's eloped with PJ.'

And she was off. Mary had to smile as she heard Angel sing in the distance:

'Here comes the bride ... ' and Jemma giving the usual response: '... Fair, fat and wide.' And then the front door slammed shut behind them, and Mary herself sat, ready to finish off the toast rather than let it go to waste.

Debbie was, in fact, with Kelly, and they were both busy popping leaflets through letter boxes in an up-market Newcastle street, though it was obvious that Debbie wasn't exactly thrilled to be doing the job.

'What time is it?'

Kelly checked her recent birthday present, pleased to have been given the opportunity.

'Nearly eight.'

With a purposeful air, Debbie closed the flap on the leaflet pouch she carried.

'Right. I'm off. I've not had me breakfast yet and I'm starving.'

Kelly was quite enjoying the quiet camaraderie of their early morning stroll of the streets, so wasn't so keen to call it a day.

'Let's just finish this street first.'

Debbie made no sign of being willing to do so.

'I still think we're bonkers doing it.'

Kelly thought about it and then had the answer.

'Winston says it's a great idea.'

But that argument didn't wash with Debbie.

'If Winston thinks it's such a brilliant idea, why isn't Winston here doing it himself?'

Kelly said it with a certain pride, after all if he wasn't really her boyfriend, at least everyone knew they were quite close.

'He's got something else important on.'

Debbie was suitably sarcastic.

'Proper little busy bee, isn't he?'

'Well, it's better than when he was moping around all over the place after Gill died now, isn't it?'

And Debbie realising she was right of course felt guilty enough to at least finish the street with her.

'Right. Let's get done then. I'm starving.'

If they both could have seen what Winston was getting up to they might not have been quite so impressed. Winston was riding Speedy's bike, while a shattered Speedy was running alongside. Speedy had decided that the first half hour of any training session wasn't bad; but beyond that it was murder. They'd been at it for near enough forty-five minutes now and Speedy was double shattered. Worst of all he had realised, away from the safety of his books, thoughts of Charlie could run riot.

Winston's occasional jolly remarks from the comfort of the bike didn't help.

'Aren't you glad I got you out now?'

'No.'

'You want to win, don't you, man?'

Speedy tried to picture it, but Charlie's angry face again clouded the view.

'Wanting to doesn't mean I will. I never win 'owt, me. Not games; not girls; not anything.'

And the thoughts having intruded with a vengeance, Speedy ran even faster so the hurt of the agonising lung-burning activity would take over and wipe them out for good.

Winston was caught out and left behind.

'Hey! Hang on, man! You'll have me exercising as well if you don't go careful!'

Speedy having finally run himself into the ground, paused at the corner of two streets gasping for breath, and waited for Winston to catch up. As Winston arrived, round the corner trundled a milk float that stopped near them.

Out of one side popped the milkman who headed for a nearby house, a clutch of bottles in his hand, and out of the other side came Danny.

He called to a gasping Speedy.

'Hi, Speedy.'

Speedy could only manage a wave.

Winston spoke for both of them.

'Hiya. Didn't know you did this.'

'Milkman needed a hand, he's pulled his back and can't manage the crates. It's a few extra quid.'

Winston viewed the wares on display.

'Couldn't flog us a bottle of that cow juice, could you?'

'Sure. Thirty-four p.'

Winston took the bottle that Danny handed him.

'Pay the man, Speedy.'

Through his gasping Speedy managed to get it out.

'Why me?'

'You're the one whose muscles need the calcium.'

Danny smiled as he said it: 'Bones.'

Winston looked blank. 'What?'

'Calcium builds bones, not muscle. Want me to put it back in the crate?'

'Naw. He needs them building as well. Going to be a right little Schwarzenegger when I've done with him, aren't you, Speedy?'

The look of Speedy as he finally sat exhausted on a nearby wall and looked for change in his tracksuit, gave the lie to Winston's high ambitions.

Danny said: 'What you up to anyhow?'

It was Winston who answered.

'Training.' He crossed to get the money off Speedy and give him the milk bottle, and then passed the money on to Danny.

'There you go.'

Speedy had hardly lifted the bottle before Winston was nagging once more.

'Come on, Speedy! Let's be having you!'

Having finished her toast, Mary had popped on her coat and made her way somewhat earlier than usual to Byker Grove, for her morning cleaning session. She soon had the vacuum cleaner out and was busily giving the place a good going at. She had just finished the hallway and was heading for the office, when she heard Alison on the telephone, and switched the machine off temporarily to give Alison a chance to hear herself speak.

'No, there are no forms to fill in, they can just roll up any time after three-thirty. I'm Alison. Tell them to ask for me... Don't worry, Mrs Bewick, I'm sure Marcus and Amanda won't have any problem making friends here. That's what Byker Grove is all about... It is; lovely place. 'Bye.'

As Alison put down the phone Mary was at the door.

'All right if I do in here, pet?'

'Yes, carry on, Mary. Bit early today?'

Mary decided to share the secret.

'I want to get done early, it's my Day Centre afternoon.'

Alison watched as Mary lugged the heavy industrial vacuum into the room behind her with one hand.

'I only wish I had half your energy.' Alison then stood ready to go off to the kitchen.

'Cup of tea?'

'No, I want to get done in here first. I don't want him tutting while I vacuum round him.'

Alison smiled at the thought of Geoff 'tutting'.

'You needn't worry. Geoff won't be in for a while yet. He's gone to a meeting.'

'Oh well, in that case a tea would go down very nicely.'

And as Alison headed for the kitchen the vacuum cleaner was blasting out once more, with Mary happily singing above the racket.


At the Town Hall, Geoff was much less cheery. He was meeting Ian McDowell, Chairman of the Council Finance Committee, who had been delegated to give Geoff the bad news. As ever the council's finances were in a parlous state; and whenever cuts were imminent, the old Byker Grove building looked like a good possible source of quick revenue.

'I'm sorry, Geoff, man. To coin a phrase, this hurts us as much as it hurts you.'

Geoff shook his head in disbelief.

'I doubt it, Ian.'

'Give me a break. If you knew what a fight I've put up.'

At which Geoff had to relent slightly. One thing was sure, Ian was on their side, and had been a good friend over the years.

'Yeah. I do, mate. You at least have.'

'We all have, whether you were aware of it or not. The entire committee. But it's out of our hands.'

Geoff thought about it before speaking.

'I can't say I didn't see the writing on the wall. Still I appreciate the early warning.'

'Least I could do.'

'So. What happens now?'

'With luck nothing for a bit.'

'So there's still hope?'

Ian didn't want to hold out too much hope, but decided his warning could be tempered.

'Same as I said. It's not official yet.'

Geoff quickly clutched at the straw on offer.

'Many a slip, right?'

Ian smiled to take the edge of it.

'Don't hold your breath.'

'I shan't.'

Geoff realised there was one more thing he had to get clear.

'And the kids? Time to break the news yet?'

Ian had no hesitation.

'I'd hang fire on that one. Officially you don't know a dickey-bird.'

Leaving the Town Hall, Geoff had a choice of jumping in the car and getting back to the Grove, or taking a stroll and contemplating the matter. The stroll won. He meandered along past the new cinema complex wondering how much it was losing every week, and headed for the underpass that would take him to the other side of the street and onward to the little hidden garden square he knew. Not big enough to be considered a park, but offering moments of peace, and a chance to think, away from the scurrying midday rush of people and traffic.

He was down the underpass stairs and about to move on, when his eyes were drawn to a scruffy boy, with a pinched face, who sat huddled with a piece of cardboard beside him with a message on it.

An old lady was leaning forward to read the message, which

Geoff could clearly see from where he stood. It said: 'Hungry and homeless, please help.' And Geoff knew the card was a lie.

The boy was Lee, one of the latest entrants to Byker Grove, who at his interview a couple of weeks before, had not only turned up neat and suited, but had talked at great length about his home life and family as well. As the old woman continued to look shortsightedly at the plaque, the boy spoke in a desperate whine.

'Spare a copper, missus ... I've not had 'owt to eat since yesterday.'

The woman said, 'Oh the poor young thing,' under her breath and reached for her purse, but Geoff's words cut through the quiet of the tunnel and echoed its length.

'It's all right, madam, I wouldn't bother. He's with me.'

Startled, the woman looked up. And seeing the authoritarian figure of Geoff decided to leave well alone and continued on her way. Lee's eyes on seeing who spoke, had taken on the look of a cornered rat. He looked beyond Geoff to the stairs, and then to the tunnel along which the woman was making her way. Again Geoff's voice boomed.

'The choice is yours, son. Run or face up to it.'

And then Geoff saw that Lee had resigned himself to facing the music.

Geoff pointed to the plastic bag that Lee was resting against.

'What's in there?'

'My school uniform.'

'Well. Put it on and get to school. I'll see you at the Grove tonight. My office, five o'clock sharp; and whatever it is I'm sure it's going to be interesting.'

And with that Geoff turned and walked back up the stairs and headed along the streets to where he'd parked the car. The thought of a nice pleasant walk had been soured in his mind.

School out of the way for the day, Speedy was once more under the iron discipline of Winston the trainee trainer, who had insisted on time trials from the entrance of Byker to where Kelly stood taking a note of the speeds halfway up the drive. Speedy raced it as fast as his pumping heart and throbbing calves would allow, screeching to a halt alongside Kelly. Panting he looked at her as she checked the figures on the stopwatch. She finally called:

'He knocked thirteen seconds off it that time, Winston.'

But Winston wasn't having any slacking.

'Not enough. Again.'

Speedy cycled back down the path at speed once more, and as he swept round a bush to head the last hundred metres to the Grove gates, two kids who he didn't know had to leap to either side of the path to avoid being mown down. The boy called at Speedy angrily.

'Hey watch it!' and the girl yelled, 'Speed freak!'

But as they split and he rode between them, all he could think to say was 'Ta,' in passing.

They both stopped, turned, and watched Speedy come to a halt with a scream of brakes by the gate. And it was the girl who finally said it for both of them.

'So this is the place Mummy said was going to be so friendly and welcoming?'

The boy simply nodded.

'It would appear so, Amanda, it would appear so.' And as one they turned and continued to walk up the path.


In the office Geoff was not being exactly forthcoming with the news he'd got from Ian McDowell that morning. Both Alison and him had been busy about their various tasks during the day, but now having finally ended up in the office together, a quiet moment before the chaos of the evening got underway, she decided it was time she knew what was going on.

'Well?'

Geoff looked up from the letter he was reading, his face asking the obvious question – 'What?'

'Are you going to tell me what happened at the Town Hall this morning, or do I guess?' Geoff put down the letter and smiled.

'Have a stab at it.'

'They're going to build us a heated swimming pool?'

'Close.'

'They're going to...' But she stopped mid-sentence as she saw Geoff's eyes harden.

He was looking at the open doorway behind her. She turned to look and saw it was the new boy Lee who was standing there. Geoff quietly spoke the code that asked her to leave the room, and leave him alone with any person who happened to be present.

'I'll talk to you later then, Alison.' And getting the message, she nonchalantly stood as if she had been about to leave in any case, and gathered a few papers together to take with her.

'Sure.'

With that she went, hearing Geoff speak coldly to Lee as she exited.

'Shut the door.'

And as the door closed she wondered what the boy had been up to.


Inside the office Geoff didn't offer Lee a seat as he usually would to any other kid on the carpet.

'You turned up then.'

'You didn't give me much choice, did you?'

'I gave you lots of choice. Sensibly you took this course, and if you play your cards right you might even still be welcome here when I've finished with you.'

Geoff left space for Lee to add anything he might want to, but there was nothing forthcoming.

'Make a habit of it, do you? Bunking off school?'

A shrug was the only reply. Geoff pressed on.

'And the begging routine? Is that a habit too?' He then got the remark in quick before Lee could do it again. 'And don't shrug. I don't like it.'

Lee rubbed his nose before he replied, to Geoff a dead give-away that a lie was coming, before the lie was even spoken.

'First time.'

Geoff's voice as he continued was icy.

'I'll tell you something about me, shall I? I'm a bit too long in the tooth for fairy stories.'

Without being asked Lee had another crack at it.

'It was a dare, see. Some kids dared me.'

And Geoff didn't believe a word of it.

'I know this much, son. First time or not it's definitely the last. Do I make myself clear?'

Lee looked down at the carpet as Geoff continued.

'I don't suppose it would break your heart if I banned you from this place. But I dare say you wouldn't be best pleased if I informed your school, your parents, and the authorities about your sneaky little games. Last time, you hear?'

'All right.'

Geoff wanted to hear him say it.

'All right what?'

He looked up.

'It's the last time.'

'Good. Make sure it is.'

Geoff turned from looking at him, and picked up a letter from the desk. Lee was bemused.

'Is that it?'

Geoff didn't look round.

'For the present.'

'You're not banning us then?'

Geoff glanced at him, his cool tone still showing no sign of thawing, this was one Byker Grover he was going to keep a firm and unremitting watch on.

'On the contrary. I want you where I can keep an eye on you, and I've got very good eyesight, sunshine. Can see over the whole of Newcastle on a fine day. Understand?'

And Lee did. He paused momentarily, and then, knowing he was dismissed, left the room, closing the door behind him, and walked straight into Spuggie who, uninvited, launched straight into it.

'You've been found out, haven't you?'

Having come out of the frying pan he had no wish to go straight into the fire so played it dim.

'Dunno what you mean.'

Spuggie didn't mince her words.

'Begging. Geoff only shuts the door when he's telling you off.'

He tried to push past but she moved to block him off.

'You're off your trolley,' he said to her.

Spuggie almost spat the words back at him.

'I know what you did 'cos Fraser told me.'

'Oh aye? And did he tell you the rest of it?'

'Yes, he did.'

'Yeah? About who was begging right alongside me?'

Spuggie had to fight now to get her temper in control before she spoke. To think that this creep could sink so low as to try to use an ill mother against someone. Finally she replied with, in the circumstances, amazing dignity.

'If you mean our mam, yes, he did. She's convalescing now. She's doing okay. But at least she had the excuse she was ill. Whereas you, you're just sick!'

And with that she turned and went off to the loo where chances were, Spuggie thought, the air would be a bit fresher.


Nicola and Charlie had settled comfortably into Nicola's bed-room at the Dobsons' having an early evening make-up session for no particular reason at all. They weren't even going to Dimmoro's café which, since the arrival of pianist Danny, had become a regular hangout.

Charlie having finished her latest effort turned to Nicola for comment.

'What do you think?'

Nicola finished putting on a layer of bright purple mascara before turning to look.

'Bit OTT?'

Charlie looked at herself in the mirror, and had to agree.

'Yes. Could be right.'

As she reached for a tissue and cream to get rid of the excess prior to having another experiment, Nicola explained the presence of the vast assortment of make-up.

'Most of this junk's Donna's from when she used to stay.'

Charlie carried on taking off the eye-shadow as she spoke.

'I've not seen her around lately. Not that I've missed her.'

'I don't see her myself so much.'

'I thought you two were practically joined at the hip.'

'We used to be. When we weren't scratching each other's eyes out.'

Both girls laughed at the memory of how they used to be when they were kids a few months back.

'She's changed.'

'Can only be for the better. She couldn't get any worse.'

'Not better or worse. Just different. We don't seem to have anything to say to each other any more.'

A silence suddenly sat between them as the reality of what Donna had been through struck both of them. Her dad Jim had nearly died after an accident at the pub and Donna, being the same blood group as he was, had moved heaven and earth to give him the kidney she thought he needed, then it turned out he didn't need it at all. And even worse, it looked as though Donna had been seeking glory for herself, when in fact she hadn't, she just wanted to help prevent her dad being an invalid for life.

If that wouldn't change you, make you grow up a bit, what would?

But the moment wasn't right for such a serious subject.

It was Charlie who finally broke the silence as Nicola finished her eyes.

'That one's good on you.'

Nicola was pleased.

'Think so?'

'Yes.'

It wasn't really that good, Charlie thought, but it did get the conversation moving on less dangerous ground again.

And so the evening continued, make-up; comment; clean up; try again, interspersed with libellous conversation about the alleged plastic surgery of the stars from Madonna to Julia Roberts via that old favourite Michael Jackson.

It was Nicola who finally voiced her horror at the thought. 'What the heck do they all do it for?!'

'Kids of twelve are having cosmetic surgery in the States now,' said Charlie as she tried the black lipstick.

Nicola gave her her full attention, aghast. 'You're joking!'

'I'm not. Their parents buy it 'em.' Then in a beautiful American accent Charlie said:

'Why sure, Darleen honey, of course you can have a nose job for your thirteenth birthday. You get much bigger child, and we can give you a boob job for your fourteenth as well.'

Nicola fell about laughing.

'Totally insane.'

It was at that point that Mary opened the door and popped her head in.

'Thought I heard you two. I've just put the kettle on. Would you like a cup of tea?'

Nicola said it for both of them.

'Lovely. Thanks, Gran.' Then a thought struck her. 'How was the Day Centre?'

Momentarily sidetracked Mary came fully into the room.

'I didn't go in the end. It's not like it used to be.'

Charlie recognised the edge of sadness in Mary's voice.

'Why not?'

'It's council cuts, you see, pet. They're in a bad way, poor souls, the old folk, and I can't think of who to turn to for help. Even the telly's broken down now, they used to enjoy their afternoon programmes.'

Charlie said it without thinking.

'There's other things besides TV.'

Mary put her right.

'Not so much when you're getting on and your old bones aren't as spry as they used to be, pet. I'm one of the lucky ones.'

Nicola was perplexed.

'I thought they used to have outings and things?'

'No money for that now. We only used to pay a pound or so each, the council subsidised the rest. Now they all just sit around all day.' She smiled at the thought before speaking it. 'Maybe I should take our Debbie and Jemma round there. They'd certainly liven them up. If they didn't finish them off first.'

Charlie's face lit up as the thought struck her.

'You know what, Mary, that's a great idea. Forget the tea; Nicola and I are off.'

Nicola was as surprised as her gran. 'Where?'

'Dimmoro's café. Time the Grovers went back into show business.'

Outside Byker, Debbie and Tessa were on the doorstep enjoying the last of the sun as Jemma and Angel at a loose end came out to join them. Jemma was about to speak when Debbie stood and turned her back to the pathway.

'Don't look!'

Jemma was totally perplexed and spoke as she looked for whatever it could be that she was supposed not to look at.

'Why not?'

'I don't want him to know I'm talking about him, do I? He gives us the creeps.'

Jemma was even more bemused. 'We weren't talking about anyone; we've just come out.'

It was Tessa who cleared up one mystery.

'No. But me and Debbie were.'

But her next remark simply added to it.

'How do you know he was begging, Deb?'

Jemma and Angel exchanged a glance. This was good stuff.

'Spuggie told us. Geoff found out and slaughtered him.'

Then Jemma saw who it must be.

'You mean that new kid Lee?!'

Debbie shouted it in a whisper.

'I said don't look!'

Angel and Jemma had a good stare at him in the distance before Jemma asked the obvious.

'So how come he's still here?'

It was Tessa who had the answer to that one.

'Probably nobody else'll have him.'

Jemma was amazed.

'I don't see why. He's not that bad.'

Angel as ever echoed Jemma.

'No. Not that bad.'

Debbie was suitably scornful.

'Do us a favour! He's gruesome.'

And as Jemma and Angel once more gave him a good staring at, he turned, saw them looking, and gave a wave in their

23

direction. As they waved back on automatic, Debbie said it furiously:

'Stupid! Now he'll know we're talking about him!'

Jemma stood. 'Come on, Angel; let's go and have a chat, see if there's any money in begging.'

And as they moved off Debbie screamed out:

'Jemma, you keep away from him!'

In the office Geoff finally let Alison know the harsh reality of the situation facing the Grove. She looked at him a long time, aghast, before she could bring herself to ask the question.

'So what's going to happen?'

Geoff looked out of the window to the view beyond. Then said it calmly.

'Lap of the God's time, love.'

She shook her head disbelievingly.

'It's not like you to be so resigned.'

Geoff turned back to look at her.

'I can fight McDowell. I can fight the Finance Committee. But I can't fight the whole blimmin' council.'

'Why not?'

Geoff smiled.

'Geoff and Goliath, aye?'

What Alison then had to say was true enough.

'Well. The little one won that time.'

But Geoff was on a downer.

'He had a miracle on his side.'

And Alison finally realised it was a truly serious situation.

In the tea bar the new kids Marcus and Amanda had settled down by themselves with coffees and Fraser, as befits a Grove employee, was doing his best to make them feel at home; but he was finding it an uphill struggle. Having discovered they were fresh from Kenya he tried the obvious.

'Did you go on safari?'

There was quite a pause before Marcus said it. 'Several times.'

Fraser smiled. 'I'd love to do that.' And his smile died as the conversation ended dead once more. He was about to make his excuses and move on when out of the blue Amanda chimed in.

'I saw a lion kill a zebra once.'

At the thought of it Fraser's stomach flipped over.

'It was horrible. The guide said, "But it's nature, miss," And I said, "I know but I still don't like watching it." It was crying. It took ages to die.'

The silence once more descended, and Fraser finally managed to find the words.

'Fascinating. Well – I really must be getting on.'

And with that he was heading for the door. He passed with Winston, who was heading for the far corner of the tea bar where Kelly was sitting nursing the last of her ice cream in the pot so she could drink the dregs down, calling as he went.

'Did you and Debbie deliver all the leaflets?'

'Yup. Did you ask Geoff's permission?'

Winston shook his head. 'Plenty of time.'

Kelly was aghast.

'It's tomorrow, man.'

'I've told you, quit worrying! It'll be okay.'

Kelly knew different. When Geoff found out he was going to explode if he hadn't been forewarned. She drained the ice cream dregs then stood.

'Let's go and tell him now!'


Jemma had Lee under none too gentle inquisition, with Angel agreeing in the usual fashion.

'Why were you begging?'

'Who told you?'

'I get to know everything, me.'

Angel nodded wisely.

'She does.'

'So? What did you do it for?'

'Dosh. What else?'

'I mean why? Are you poor?'

'Nothing to do with it.'

'Did you make loads?'

'None of your blinkin' business.'

'I bet you did. I bet you made yourself look dead pathetic. Did you cough a lot? You should have done.'

Jemma demonstrated her pathetic beggar-boy cough as Lee asked the question.

'Why you so interested?'

'I've never met no beggars before.'

Angel nodded.

'Me neither.'

'I'm not a blimmin' beggar, will you get that!'

Jemma knew why.

'So what will you do instead of begging now Geoff's stopped that?'

'Even if I knew, I'm hardly likely to tell you now, am I?'

'Doesn't matter. I'll find out anyway. I've told you. I find out everything, me.'

And for the last time Angel nodded.

'Yeah. She does.'


Marcus and Amanda had taken the risk of going their separate ways for a while and Marcus was doing quite well in the chat stakes. Duncan and Speedy who he'd crossed to sit with, were happy to let him know of the big forth-coming event.

'So when is this race then?'

Speedy was the one to answer as he was sort of the star turn.

'Next Saturday.'

'And you're the favourite, right?'

'They seem to think I'm in with a chance; yeah.'

Duncan chipped in cheerfully while Speedy glowed gently in the background.

'He's miles better than that wally the Denton Burn's lot are putting up. Talk about guided missile.'

Marcus smiled at the thought.

'I know. We had him shooting up our backsides like a Scud on the way in.' Marcus directed his remark at Speedy, and Lee arriving to escape further questioning from Jemma and Angel, overheard and was immediately all ears. 'Might have a few quid on you,' Marcus continued, 'if anyone's taking bets. I never say no to a sure thing.'

Duncan was suitably impressed.

'You do it a lot then?'

'Used to go to the Ngong races nearly every weekend in Nairobi.'

Whilst Marcus felt he was doing fairly well considering he was a new boy, Amanda felt she couldn't put a foot right.

She started off talking with Tessa and Debbie, who seemed set on asking really stupid questions and then answering themselves.

Debbie started it, talking to Tessa as though Amanda wasn't there.

'Do they have cars and that?'

'Of course they have cars. What do you think? They go about on donkey carts?'

'Well it's Africa, isn't it?'

Amanda tried to put her right. 'Kenya actually.'

Debbie was flummoxed.

'That's Africa.'

'East Africa.'

As Debbie was so obviously thick she tried talking to Tessa.

'I don't know where you come from.'

'Sierra Leone.'

And Amanda was immediately on safer ground.

'Ah. That's West Africa.'

Or so she thought, but Tessa was obviously nettled.

'I know where it is.'

Debbie joined in again.

'Hey, Mandy – are there snakes? Did you have to sleep in mosquito nets?'

'Not in Nairobi. And it's Amanda if you don't mind.'

Amanda didn't need a translator to tell her what the look that Tessa and Debbie exchanged meant.

Meanwhile Marcus had been joined by Lee, who had waited till Speedy and Duncan moved off before going over to him.

'If you went to the races a lot I expect you know all about taking bets?'

'Point of fact I used to run a book at school. Strictly ...'
Marcus tapped his nose indicating Lee should keep it to himself,
'... of course.'

Lee tapped his own nose in reply.

'Say no more.' Then got down to the real business. 'Thought
about having a bash with this cycle run?'

'Opening a book?'

'Make a few quid.'

'I don't do it for money.'

'What for then?'

'Excitement. Pitting my wits against the odds. Anyway – why
me? Why not you?'

Lee shook his head.

'Keeping a low profile for the moment. Geoff's got his eye
on me. As a new boy you could probably get away with it,
mind.'

'I'd have to study the field first, find out the form.'

'No problem. I've got all the info here.'

Lee took a sheet of paper out of his pocket and passed it to a
surprised Marcus.

'How'd you manage that?'

Lee smiled his crooked little smile.

'Been spending some time in the shrubbery with a stopwatch
round at Denton Burn's. So what do you think?'

'As I said, I'll think about it.'

And Lee knew Marcus would do it.

All he'd got to do now was make sure he bet on the winner,
and he knew a pretty good way of guaranteeing that.


In Dimmoro's café Charlie and Nicola told Danny what they
had in mind.

'You remember the show we were going to do?'

'The one Geoff blew out of the water, and quite right too.'

Charlie rose to the bait nicely.

'He wasn't right!'

Danny had to smile that the wind-up was going so well.

'Come on, Charlie, it was a duff show and you know it.'

Nicola took over.

'Only because we didn't have enough time to get it into shape.'

Danny finally saw what was coming; they wanted to do it again at the old people's Day Centre.

'Oh no!'

Charlie couldn't see the problem.

'Why not? We wouldn't be charging anything, we'd do it for free.'

'Only way you'd get an audience!'

Nicola spelt it out.

'How would you like to be old and frail and stuck inside with nothing to do and a broken telly?'

Danny still wasn't convinced.

'What makes you think they'd want us?'

'Gran thinks they would. She thinks it's a great idea.'

'Oh well! If Gran thinks so . . .'

At that point Greg, Charlie's former boyfriend, was passing by, and seeing Charlie through the café window, popped his head in the doorway to call in her direction.

'Hey, Superstar! Can we come to your farewell party?'

Charlie, seeing who it was, didn't waste words.

'Push off.'

But Nicola wanted to know more.

'What farewell party?'

'When they close down the Grove.'

Nicola, Charlie and Danny said it in unison, shocked. 'What!?'

'Haven't you heard? They're knocking it down. Building a block of luxury flats or something. Best thing that could happen to the dump.'

And with that he had gone leaving them with nothing to do but stare at each other aghast, as the message sunk home.

The Grove was to be closed down.

# CHAPTER TWO

It was eight o'clock in the morning at the Dobsons' and Nicola was searching for the source of a strange rhythmical noise that had awakened her from her sleep. Finding that the sound came from Debbie and Jemma's room she flung open the door, and there was a sight she could hardly believe.

Debbie was on the dressing table manically tap dancing. Nicola watched her amazed.

'What the heck you doing up there?'

Debbie kept the rhythm going as she replied.

'You can't do taps on a carpet.'

'Serve you right if you fall off and break your silly little neck. Waking up the whole house.'

Debbie having finished the routine with a suitable flourish climbed down.

'It's for your show. Besides, clever clogs, Mam and Dad are already up and she's dead to the world.'

She pointed at the duvet covered blob in the second bed. Jemma's voice floated up from a gap. 'No, I'm not. Just hiding from the racket.'

As it turned out Debbie was right about their parents. Their mum Kath was in her dressing gown in the kitchen making herself a coffee, and Alan was just coming in from the garden, togged out in his gardening clothes. She looked at him as he entered.

'You're another one up early.'

Alan crossed to the sink to rinse his hands as he spoke.

'Aye. I wanted to get the rest of the dahlias lifted. Be dark when I get back. Couldn't you sleep?'

Kath sat down at the table with her cup before replying.

'We can't put off telling the girls forever.'

Debbie just arriving overheard.

'Telling the girls what?'

Alan shook his head in disbelief at the quality of Debbie's hearing.

'Ye Gods, Kath! Were there bats in your family, the ears on this one.'

Debbie wasn't to be sidetracked that easily.

'Tell us what, Mam?'

Kath shook her head. 'Later, pet.'

She noticed Debbie was still wearing her tap shoes.

'Going to school like that, are you?'

As she spoke Debbie launched into her routine again on the linoleum covered floor.

'This floor's the only place I can practise.'

Alan smiled as he watched her get under way, speaking for his own benefit.

'Ginger Rodgers, eat your heart out.'

Jemma also arriving at the doorway asked the obvious.

'Who's Ginger Rodgers?'

At which Alan shook his head in disbelief once more.

'The whole family has ears like bats!'

At that moment a pretty young girl in skin-tight shiny black Lycra shorts and top with pink and yellow flashings, was running along by the riverbank. Totally lost in the music of her Walkman, she didn't see Speedy passing on his bike, but seeing her he nearly ended up in the river as he was so busy watching her he didn't see a bump in the track and nearly went flying.

A little while later the girl also didn't see the young scruffy-looking man watching her as she passed.

He stayed where he was for a moment, and then having ran his hand over the stubble on his chin thoughtfully, he came to a decision, and leapt up to race after her.

In a street parallel with the river, Danny and the milkman were just coming to the end of the round. The milkman had crossed to the far side of the street, and Danny had just taken a bottle out of the crate, when he heard a horrified scream pierce the morning air, and Danny was off racing in the direction of the scream, still clutching the bottle in his hand.

Reaching the tow path, he saw the girl in Lycra shorts

struggling with a man who was trying to rip the gold chain from her neck, as she fought against him getting it.

Danny called from where he was:

'Hey you, stop that!' then ran to where they were still struggling.

Danny grabbed the young man by the shoulder, swung him round and lifted the milk bottle menacingly.

'I said leave her alone – if you don't want this over your head.'

Ignoring the threat the man punched Danny to the ground, sending the milk bottle flying, and leapt on him. Without hesitation, the girl flung herself onto his back, pummelling him as hard as she could, and in seconds the man had had enough. Struggling free from her grip he ran off, with the girl calling the single word after him.

'Yob!'

Danny got himself back on his feet.

'What happened?'

'He was after this.'

She showed him the gold chain and locket at her throat.

'No way was he getting it.'

Danny wasn't too sure about that.

'You'd have had a job stopping him in the end.'

'What do you mean! I did!' She was defiant. 'Wimps like him don't scare me.'

'All the same . . . '

'All the same what?!' she answered defensively.

As she spoke he tried not to look at her figure that was moulded by the outfit she was wearing, but couldn't stop himself. The sexist remark didn't help her temper.

'You shouldn't go out on your own dressed like that. Not this hour of the morning.'

She was suitably amazed and angry.

'It's running gear. What's wrong with it?'

'Nothing. Well, it is a bit . . . ' He couldn't bring himself to say the word so she said it for him.

'. . . *provocative*? Well, tough. All you lads are the same. Only one thought in your mucky little heads.'

'I'm just saying how it strikes some people.'

He could see she was getting really angry with him.

'I'm not going out in blimmin' bin liners just 'cos of pathetic specimens like him.'

'He might have been a lot bigger than you ... and a lot stronger ... and after more than your necklace.'

She couldn't help but smile as the thought struck her.

'And you mightn't have been there to come to me rescue with your trusty bottle of semi-skimmed.'

On automatic pilot Danny had picked up the bottle from where it had fallen without breaking when the man punched him, and now he realised he was holding it over his shoulder like a weapon.

Miffed that she could take the mickey after he had come to her rescue, he decided to get back to work.

'I'll leave you to get on with your run. I've got to get back.'

As he set off she called after him.

'Hey. What's your name?'

Danny kept walking as he called back.

'Danny.'

'Nice meeting you, Danny.'

As she ran on once more Danny said to himself sarcastically:

'And thanks for your help.'

In the Byker office Geoff contemplated the happenings of the last couple of days. He'd managed to placate the kids when the news of the possible closure had spread through the building like wild fire. He was saved from having to tell a lie in the end, because of a comment from Spuggie, to Charlie, Danny and Nicola.

'If it was Denton Burn kids who said it – it must be a lie.'

And when PJ had asked Geoff, he'd simply said:

'You heard the lady.'

And then he'd sidetracked them by instantly agreeing to the concert in the old people's Day Centre, instead of arguing as usual.

As the telephone rang in the office, he was thinking about Winston, Debbie and Kelly's idea to earn money for Gill's memorial, which he had thought at the time hadn't been a bad one.

Trouble was it had turned out to be a disaster in the end.

They had leafleted the area offering a cheap, early-morning car wash at the Grove and the popularity of the offer had caused heavy traffic jams. One of those who couldn't get through for a long time had been Ian McDowell. When he finally did get through the news was a bombshell – it was confirmed the Grove was to be closed.

When Geoff picked up the phone, it was Ian again, and the news was equally appalling. He wanted to bring a group of possible buyers round.

'What time?'

Geoff listened to make sure he'd heard right the first time. He had.

'But it's smack in the middle of the afternoon, Ian; the kids will all be here ... Yes, I know businessmen are busy people but ...'

He let Ian get it off his chest once more, and then finally gave in.

'Okay. Just means I shall have to tell them sooner than I planned, that's all ... I didn't see any point in upsetting them till it was definite ...'

He let Ian finish his apologies.

'Well, see you four-thirty then.'

Geoff replaced the telephone carefully, while thinking about it. He was now going to have to break the news to the Grovers that the rumours were right after all. And that was one message he could well do without giving.

Outside the Gallaghers', Spuggie and Speedy were busily working on Speedy's bike, while Winston sat on the wall and supervised. He pointed out a dull patch to Spuggie.

'You missed a bit there.'

She stood and offered him the polishing cloth.

'Here, you do it then.'

Winston immediately backed off.

'No. You're doing a good job. Carry on.'

She knelt back down and got on with it once more, as Winston spoke again, directing his remark at Speedy.

'Though I still think you should have taken it to a bike shop.'

Speedy smiled happily.

'When I've finished with it, Winston, it'll be purring like a kitten.'

Winston wasn't having that.

'It's roaring like a tiger we want, man, if we're to stand half a chance.'

Speedy paused and looked at him.

'What's with this *we*? I'm the one that's blimmin' riding it.'

Just then he saw Lee approaching.

'Hey-up.'

Winston and Spuggie looked in the indicated direction. By the time Lee arrived all three were intent on other things.

Lee was indifferent to their coolness, calling the greeting cheerfully enough as he passed. 'Hiya. Wish you all the best for Saturday, man.'

Speedy kept polishing. 'Ta,' he said.

As Lee walked on, Winston looked at his disappearing back. 'Creep.'

Spuggie also said it, heartfelt without looking up. 'Double creep.'

And Speedy being Speedy leapt to the underdog's defence.

'He did wish us luck for the race.'

Silence fell as they worked on for a while, then Speedy had a thought.

'Just say I do win it. Girls like winners, don't they?'

Winston and Spuggie exchanged a glance and then looked at Speedy. He got the message.

'Just a thought.'


By four o'clock the Grove was awash with activity. The idea of doing a show at the Day Centre had really caught on. Debbie and Tessa were tap dancing in one corner; Amanda and Marcus were practising a ventriloquist act, while Charlie was singing through the Speedy/Danny song, with Danny at the piano.

In another corner Duncan was practising magic tricks while Angel and Jemma fought over who should be the magician's assistant this time.

Meanwhile PJ was here, there and everywhere, letting everybody know he was back in charge once more. He called to Charlie in passing.

'Still got to project more, Charlie. I don't want the wrinklies thinking I represent rubbish.'

As ever she gave as good as she got.

'Any more comments, Mr Impresario, and I'll project you right out of this room.'

PJ shook his head amazed as he went.

'Blimmin' aggressive women.'


Alison entered the room along with Fraser while the activity was at full height.

'Blimey. It's like backstage at the London Palladium in here.'

Hearing the remark PJ said it for all of them.

'We're not having Geoff slag us off again, Alison. This time we get it right.'

Fraser smiled.

'Good on ya, PJ.'

At that PJ caught sight of Debbie and Tessa seriously intent on getting a tricky step right.

'Teeth and smiles, girls! Don't forget – teeth and smiles!'

Alison saw that Kelly wasn't joining in.

'You not doing anything, Kelly?'

Kelly shook her head.

'No. I'm useless, me. I can't sing or dance or 'owt.'

Fraser thought he had the answer.

'You could tell some jokes.'

'I can never remember the end.'

Alison laughed.

'Me neither. I reckon some of us are just born to be spear carriers, pet.'

And Kelly nodded her head agreeably.

Lee was silently watching Marcus and Amanda's act. Marcus asked questions as the ventriloquist, and then also answered for the 'dummy' while Amanda moved her mouth in time with the words, pretending to speak.

'Can you tell me what this is?'

'Course I can, you great ganana, it's a gottle of gear.'

'I must say you're not a very good dummy, are you?'

'You mean you're not a very good ventriloquist.'

Lee waited till a suitable moment presented itself before addressing his remark at Marcus.

'About that bit of business.'

It was Amanda who answered for him.

'Go away, we're busy.' And then asked Marcus nosily, 'What business?'

Ignoring her question Marcus called to Lee: 'Later, man.'

Satisfied Lee went off, but Amanda wasn't as easily sidetracked.

'What business?' No reply forthcoming she had a guess at it. 'You're not getting up to anything stupid again, are you? You know what Dad said last time.'

Marcus's face hardened at the thought. But his remark was bravado more than anything else.

'I'm not scared of him.'


Nicola arriving late, saw Charlie and Danny at the piano and crossed straight to them.

'Sorry I'm late. How's it going?'

Danny winked at Charlie, before answering.

'Tell your gran she can relax, Nicola. I don't think we're going to disgrace her.'

Jemma, having won the job of being Duncan's assistant, was doing quite nicely till she saw Lee going out of the front door. She dropped the prop she was holding.

'Right. Time for a break.'

Duncan was amazed.

'Who says?'

Jemma heading for the door called it.

'I do.'

'You can't just stop halfway through a trick!'

Angel piped up from where she sat sulking by the wall.

'I'll help if you like, Duncan.'

Jemma turned back.

'No, you won't. I'll be back in a sec.' And then she'd gone through the door at a trot and caught up with Lee.

'Aren't you doing anything for the show?'

Lee looked to see who spoke.

'Not my scene, man.'

'We could do something together if you like.'

'Thought you were helping Houdini?'

'That's just kids' stuff.'

'Well, if it's just kids' stuff, why are you so keen to do it then?'

Duncan had come to the doorstep to call after her.

'You coming back or what, Jemma?!'

Jemma smiled at Lee.

'Because he can't manage without me. See you.'

And with that she was heading back for the door as Lee watched her go.

Geoff came into the room and crossed to stand near Fraser and Alison.

'Looks like we've got nearly a full house.'

It was Alison who said it.

'Good a time as any, eh?'

'Yeah.' With that Geoff banged on a nearby table for order.

'Right! Simmer down, please. Can I have a bit of hush.'

Slowly silence finally fell, and they could tell from Geoff's face it was serious.

'The thing is, I'm afraid I've got some bad news. And there ain't no way to sweeten this particular pill, so I'm going to give it to you straight . . .'

They each hung on his every word.


Winston, Spuggie and Speedy were walking up the path to the Grove when a big posh car overtook them full of what looked like businessmen. Speedy asked Spuggie the question.

'Who are them?'

She watched the car pass before answering.

'How the heck should I know?'

Winston was surprised.

'I thought you'd know everything now your brother's a helper.'

She decided a lie wouldn't go amiss.

'Well, even if he does tell us everything, it's in strictest confidence. I'd not go blabbing to you lot.'

Seeing the car pull up at the front of the Grove they raced to catch up so they didn't miss anything. Entering they were struck by the silence and the horrified look that was on every face. In the silence they heard the office door close behind Geoff and Alison.

Spuggie asked it first. 'What's happened?'

No reply.

Speedy asked second. 'What's up?'

And still no response forthcoming, Winston asked third.

'What's going on?'

It was Fraser who finally said it, quietly.

'They're closing the Grove.'

Winston, Speedy and Spuggie shouted in a horrified harmony:

'They're what?!'

Fraser continued.

'The council are short of funds. They're selling the building to raise money.'

Winston was adamant.

'They can't do that!'

Fraser shook his head sadly.

'They can, you know. Geoff says they're flogging it to some big property company.'

Nicola was the first one among the Grovers to get her voice back.

'*De luxe* apartments with all mod. cons . . .'

Followed by Tessa, 'That they can sell for keen prices.'

And Fraser spelt it out.

'After they've demolished this place.'

Spuggie was aghast.

'Demolish it! You're mean they're going to knock it all down? The Grove won't even be here any more?'

Alison had entered the room again as Spuggie spoke. 'I'm afraid it won't, Spug.'

Geoff was behind her acting as a tour guide for the men who had arrived in the flash car.

'This is the general activities room.' Geoff saw that all eyes were on them, and the eyes were throwing silent and deadly daggers at the smooth-suited gents he had brought in. 'Most of you know Mr McDowell from the council. And these gentlemen are from Prestige Properties. Mr Bewick, Mr Carter and Mr Dunn.'

The one called Bewick moved to the front of the group, his eyes on Marcus and Amanda who were absolutely rooted where they sat side by side. Their faces pale with horror. He called cheerfully:

'Jambo, kids!'

At the strange greeting suddenly every eye had spun round and was now on them.

'And what are you two up to here?'

It was Debbie who broke the shocked silence.

'Do you know him?!'

Marcus had to swallow hard before he could finally find his voice.

'Er . . . Sort of.'

He needn't have bothered dodging it.

'Meet my two sprogs. Marcus, my son. Amanda, my daughter.'

Once more every eye was on Marcus and Amanda, and they both sincerely wished the floor would open and swallow them up.

In homes throughout the town that night young voices were raised, and parents' ears were bent as children noisily complained.

The Dobson living room was no different to any other.

Jemma said it for the hundredth time.

'It's not rotten well fair! Where the heck are we all meant to go?'

And Debbie again gave the same reply.

'I expect they'll find us some crummy little tin hut somewhere.'

But Nicola was not to be placated.

'Even if they find us a flippin' palace it won't be the same. I've been going to the Grove since I was twelve.'

Jemma came back as an instant echo.

'So have I.'

Debbie was scathing.

'You're only twelve now.'

Jemma looked round for support and picked on Mary.

'That's not the point, is it, Gran?'

But Mary, battling with a tricky bit of knitting, wasn't having any of it.

'Don't bring me into it, pet, I've got enough troubles of my own.'

At that point Alan and Kath entered, and simply stood there. Alan gave a little cough to signal an announcement.

But Jemma ignored it, wanting the present discussion to continue.

'Dad, can't you do anything?'

Debbie laughed at the thought.

'Yeah. Get his pals at the leek society to belt them with giant leeks.'

Nicola cut cold across Debbie's laughter.

'It's not funny, Debs.'

And Debbie knew it.

'I know.'

Alan cut through the conversation as if it had never happened.

'The thing is, girls, your mam and me have something to tell you.'

Mary immediately gathered her knitting and stood.

'I shall be in my room when you've done,' she said, then headed for the door.

Debbie was bemused.

'What's she mean, "when you've done"?'

Kath smiled.

'She just being tactful, pet.'

Nicola added her thoughts.

'Why? She isn't usually. Oh heck! It's not more bad news, is it?'

For once Debbie agreed with her.

'Not twice in one day. I couldn't bear it.'

Jemma held her tummy.

'I think I'm going to be sick.'

Alan stopped the banter.

'Behave yourself, hinny. We don't think it's bad news, do we, love?'

The silence held until Nicola could stand it no more.

'What is it, Mam?'

Alan looked at Kath.

'Go on, pet. Let them know.'

And finally she did.

'We're going to have another baby.'

The silence was electric. It seemed to go on for ages, until finally Jemma just had to speak and get it off her chest.

'I think that's the most disgusting thing I've ever heard.'

And then she was running sobbing for the door, through it, and up the stairs, as the others simply stood and stared at each other speechlessly.

It was much later that evening, when the conversation continued in Debbie and Jemma's bedroom, with Nicola doing her best to placate an upset Jemma.

'I know it's a shock, Jem. It's a shock for us too.'

Jemma managed to speak through her tears.

'How can they?! A baby at their age!'

Their age wasn't a problem for Debbie.

'They're not so old. Mum's only thirty-eight.'

Jemma had a sudden thought that made her sit up with the shock of it.

'Where will it sleep? It's certainly not coming in my room.'

Debbie defended her corner.

'It's our room, if you don't mind. It wouldn't bother me. I think babies are sweet.'

Jemma lay back down again.

'I can just imagine them all at school.'

Nicola again tried to calm her down.

'You don't have to tell them. Nobody else knows apart from Gran.'

Debbie scoffed at the thought. 'You can't keep being pregnant secret, stupid.'

Nicola wasn't to be put off so easily.

'You can for a couple of months.'

'What's the point?'

Nicola thought about it.

'I'd sooner the kids at the Grove don't know yet. Just keep it between us.'

Debbie agreed.

'Yeah, okay then.'

While Jemma was just miserable.

'I wouldn't mind if we never had to tell them. It's been a revolting day, this.' And for once there was no disagreement between the three of them.

It had indeed been a truly revolting day.


Next morning in the bright sunshine, two teams of Byker Grovers were busily polishing cars in a smart Newcastle street. Duncan, who was working with Debbie and Kelly on Winston's team, suddenly feeling a touch of stage fright, had a good grumble as he polished. 'I don't know why we're doing this, Winston. We should be having a last rehearsal by rights, if we're going to get it right this afternoon.'

Kelly smiled at him.

'I shouldn't worry, Dunc. You're as good as you're ever going to get.'

And Winston chipped in.

'Which isn't very.'

Duncan made his next remark to Debbie.

'It's all right for him, he's not even in the flippin' show.'

But Debbie wasn't listening, she'd just remembered about the baby.

'Debbie?'

She looked up and saw Duncan watching her intently.

'What?'

'You upset about the news?'

She dropped her polishing cloth with the shock of it.

'What news! What do you mean!?'

'Them closing the Grove. Only – they'll find us another place; they're forced to.'

Debbie picked her cloth up as she spoke.

'Oh that. Yeah – of course,' relieved that Duncan didn't know the real reason for her being so quiet this morning.

Meanwhile down by the riverside sitting on a grassy bank, Nicola had unburdened herself about the baby news to Charlie, who sympathised.

'I suppose it must have been a bit of a shock when they told you?'

'More than a bit.'

'I don't know how I'd feel if it was me.'

'You're an only child.'

Charlie turned and looked at her, surprised.

'What's that got to do with it?'

'There's three of us already. This one'll be four.'

'I know maths isn't my strong point but I can count that far.'

Nicola was suddenly intensely serious.

'The world is already over-populated, Charlie. What would happen if everybody had four kids?'

'Everybody isn't going to, are they? I'm certainly not having any more than two. One of each. I wouldn't mind twins actually. Save a lot of messing about.'

But Nicola wasn't to be sidetracked.

'Charlie, somebody's got to make a stand.'

'Like you did with your conservationist friend, you mean.'

'Okay, so I got it wrong, but I still care about the future of this planet of ours. That's why it's so embarrassing.'

'It's your parents' problem, not yours.'

'I don't know how they can be so ... so irresponsible.'

'Lighten up, Nic, there's nothing you can do about it.'

'No.'

Then Nicola remembered her pact with Debbie and Jemma.

'Do us a favour though. Keep it to yourself? Only I just had to talk to someone. Once, it would have been Donna.'

Charlie smiled.

'Her loss, my gain.'

She stood. 'Come on, let's get to the Grove. Coach will be arriving in about an hour.'

As they stood the girl in micro Lycra gear was just jogging past. She saw them giving her a good staring at and stopped.

'What?'

Nicola said it before she could stop herself.

'Aren't you, you know ... a bit ...' In the nick of time she stopped herself saying under-dressed, '... cold?'

'What do you mean?'

It was Charlie who made the point.

'You don't seem to be wearing very much.'

'Not you two as well!'

Nicola was first bemused.

'What d'you mean?'

'Just this thug yesterday tried to steal this.'

'You mean you were attacked?'

'Not really. I gave him what for.'

Charlie was very intent.

'Did you tell anyone?'

The girl called as she continued on her way. 'No point. I can handle anything.'

Charlie shook her head.

'She's mad ...'

Nicola agreed.

'She wants to be careful. There's been a couple of things like that along here.'

Charlie looked at her.

'So what we doing here?!'

'Well there's two of us. Anyway ...' And in a perfect imitation of the girl's voice Nicola repeated her last cocky remark, '... we can handle anything.'

And laughing they were on their way.

Having finished all the cars on offer in one street, Duncan, Winston, Debbie and Kelly turned the corner and started cleaning the first car in the next street.

A bunch of Denton Burn's boys approached as they started to work. Charlie's ex boyfriend Greg was leading them. He spoke as they got started.

'Something you should know.'

Winston looked up. 'Oh yeah?'

'This is our patch.'

Winston smiled at the thought and kept right on working.

'Is that right?'

'Ask anyone.'

Kelly was equally dismissive.

'We didn't see no notice saying "Private property of Denton Burn".'

Which Duncan thought was a good point.

'No, we didn't.'

'All the same that's the way the cookie crumbles. So be good kids and move on, eh?'

The group of boys now surrounding them was slightly menacing. At that point a policeman came out of a house about halfway along the street, and turned to say goodbye to the person he'd been seeing. The boys saw him and immediately moved off, breaking up into groups of two and three as they went.

'Who said there's never a copper there when you need one?' remarked Winston.

And Debbie, Duncan and Kelly laughed as they continued to work.


In a quiet corner of the Grove grounds, Marcus had set up shop and soon the money was coming rolling in. Lee stood nearby and watched as kids arrived to place their bets.

'Looks like it was a good idea of mine.'

Marcus glanced up to see who spoke.

'Doing all right. So who do you fancy?'

'Give me your odds first.'

'All the hot money's going on Superwheels there...'

He pointed to Speedy who was a few metres away giving his bike a final polish.

'He's favourite at two to one.'

Lee sniffed at the thought.

'I don't bet on favourites, me. No percentage in it. Who else you got on offer?'

Marcus looked at his list.

'Well, there's Jamie Croft from Saint Saviours YC at nine to two; and there's a lad from Gateshead, Hamel Patel, at six to one . . .'

Lee's question came smoothly.

'What about Terry Cowgill?'

'He's from Denton Burn.'

'That mean he can't ride a bike?'

'I thought the kids from here have nothing to do with them lot?'

'I'm not planning on running alongside him feeding him barley sugar.'

'I can give you five to one.'

Lee did a quick mental calculation and then decided on his stake.

'Okay. Twenty quid.'

Marcus was amazed.

'Where do you think you are, Ascot? I'll let you put five on.'

'Make it ten and it's a deal.'

'You'll have me skint, man.'

'Haway! Bookies never lose.'

Marcus put his hand out, and Lee gave him the money, speaking as he did so.

'Five to one, right?'

'That's what you heard – and I'm a man of my word.'


At that moment Winston and co., work finished for the day, were walking up the drive. Winston was counting up the cash they had made, pleased at the amount.

'Another couple of days like today and Gill's memorial's as good as bought.'

Kelly was a bit worried about the incident in the last street.

'But what about them lads?'

Debbie agreed with her.

'You heard what they said, Winston.'

Winston was dismissive.

'We're not scared of a bunch of Denton Burner's are we, Dunc?'

While Duncan didn't quite agree, he decided to offer a change of subject rather than saying it. He pointed in Marcus's direction, where a straggle of boys were still doing business with him.

'What's going on over there?'

Winston saw where he pointed.

'Let's go find out.'

Debbie was quite shocked at the thought.

'They're never talking to him, are you?'

Winston was perplexed. 'Why not?'

'Because his dad's blimmin' knocking us down, that's why not. And the other one's well gruesome too.' She was pointing at Lee who still stood on the sidelines. But Winston wasn't to be swayed, he was dead set on finding out what the big attraction was.

'I'm only going to find out what they're up to ... Come on, Dunc.'

And as they set off in his direction, Debbie and Kelly headed for the Grove.


Winston, arriving at Marcus's side, didn't mince words.

'What's the scam?'

Marcus gave change to a young boy who was having twenty pence each way on Speedy as he spoke.

'No scam. Just a chance to make a few quid from your flying friend.'

'Yeah? How?'

'Having a bet, of course.'

Duncan said it as he moved off.

'Naw – mugs' game that.'

But Winston was suddenly aware he had a pocketful of money and to get a decent memorial he was going to need lots more.

Having gone straight to the girls' loo, Debbie was soon deep in conversation with Tessa who was there getting made-up, ready for the trip to the old people's Day Centre.

'It's not that I don't like babies, they're dead cute.'

Tessa laughed.

'Dead noisy as well.'

'Not all the time. And it might be a boy, be brilliant to have a little brother, but I'm sort of scared as well.'

Tessa was perplexed.

'What of?'

'Women die having babies, don't they?'

'Not these days.'

'But they can. Especially when they're quite old.'

'Your mum's not old.'

At that moment the conversation stopped as Amanda entered, carrying a carrier bag. She smiled when she saw them both.

'There you are. I've been looking all over for you.' She reached into the bag, and brought out two sets of tights and leotards, one purple, and one a bright and shocking pink.

Debbie looked at them coolly.

'What are those for?'

Amanda's smile was rapidly fading in the face of their cool reaction.

'For your routine this afternoon. I've hardly worn them. I thought it'd be nice if you swapped the tights round, the pink leotard with the purple tights and the . . . '

Tessa interrupted the flow.

'We've already got our outfits, thank you.'

As ever Amanda chose the wrong line.

'But they're just boring old black school tights, aren't they?'

Tessa turned to look at herself in the mirror.

'Maybe. But they're *our* boring old black school ones.'

Debbie also turned. Amanda was now looking at both their backs, knowing she was being shunned. She put the tights and leotards back in the bag and put it on the floor between them.

'Oh well. I'll leave them in case you change your minds.' And turned and left as quickly as she could.

As soon as she was gone Debbie said:

'Blimmin' cheek! As though we're a couple of charity cases.'

The minibus that was taking the Grovers to the Day Centre arrived dead on time, and Geoff was soon trying to get everyone gathered and on board.

'Come on, you lot, get a move on!'

Nicola, Charlie and Danny were first in, quickly followed by Kelly and Winston. Geoff called to Fraser who was standing watching from the Grove doorway.

'You sure you can hold the fort for a couple of hours?'

Fraser called back.

'No problem, Geoff. Looks like the place will be nearly empty anyway.'

Geoff, seeing Speedy still by his bike making a final adjustment, called to him.

'Going under your own steam, Speedy?'

Winston popped his head out of the minibus window to answer to him.

'No, he's not. He's got to conserve his energy for tomorrow, he has.'

Then called to Speedy:

'On the bus, man.'

Speedy really rather fancied a ride now the bicycle was tuned to perfection.

'Day Centre's not far. I don't mind riding.'

Winston bawled out:

'I said, *on the bus*.'

And Speedy, having finally got the managerial message, locked up his bike, and crossed to climb on board.

Amanda and Marcus stood to one side, as Amanda gave him a piece of her mind.

'I wish you wouldn't take bets, Marc. You know you got into trouble for it last time.'

'That was different. That was at school; and at least it's got some of the lads talking to me now.'

Amanda remembered how Debbie and Tessa had given her the cold shoulder.

'None of the girls are talking to me.' And she knew who to blame for that. 'It's all Dad's fault. They look at me like something you scrape off your shoe.'

And then her final request was almost a plea.

'Let's go home, Marcus. I don't want to do our act.'

'We're not running away just because of him.'

'It's not just 'cos of him though. They never liked us anyway.'

And it was at that moment, as if to confirm the point, that Debbie arrived holding Amanda's carrier bag at arm's length in front of her.

'I think you left something behind.'

As Amanda took the bag, Debbie went to get on the bus with Tessa who was waiting at the door for her. Behind them Jemma was about to board the bus with Angel when she saw Lee standing off to one side; she pushed Angel on ahead of her.

'You go on – bag a seat.'

Then she crossed to speak to Lee.

'You can sit next to us if you like.'

He watched the kids crowding on the bus disdainfully.

'I'm not going.'

'Why not? Be a laugh.'

'I've got better things to do than sit around with a bunch of old fogies.'

'Suit yourself.'

Jemma went back to the bus and diving in front of Marcus got on behind Amanda.

As Marcus was also about to get on, Spuggie was at his side.

'I'm sorry.'

Marcus looked round at her, surprised.

'What for?'

'This lot.'

She indicated the bus full of kids.

'You can't help it about your dad knocking the Grove down.'

Marcus smiled at the thought.

'He's not doing it personally. He's just the architect who draws up the plans.'

'Anyroad, I know what it's like being blamed for what your dad does. You should have heard the names local kids called us every time ours got banged up for being D. and D.'

'What's that?'

'Drunk and disorderly.'

Spuggie didn't quite know why she had made her confession of parental weakness, and suddenly worried how he would take it. She needn't have worried; he smiled at her kindly.

'Come on, Spuggie. Let's go find ourselves a seat together.'

And that was exactly what they did.

The last few stragglers having got on, Geoff also climbed on board.

'Right, if that's the lot, let's go. Can't keep the pensioners waiting!'

But suddenly Jemma jumped up from her seat beside Angel at the back and ran for the door.

'Stop! Let me off!'

Angel called after her.

'Why? Where are you going?'

'I've changed me mind. I might come on later.'

Geoff was at the doorway blocking her path.

'You don't want to stop here on your own, hinny.'

Looking out of the window Debbie saw Lee standing there.

'She won't be on her own though, will she?'

Alison put Geoff's mind at rest.

'It's okay. Fraser's here.'

Geoff moved to one side.

'Okay, Jemma pet. If that's what you want.'

Jemma was about to get off the bus when Duncan twigged what was going on.

'What about us? What about me act?! This is charming, this is.'

Jemma yelled back as she stepped down:

'Angel can do it. She's moaned on long enough about wanting to.'

As the bus finally pulled off, Jemma crossed to where Lee stood. He spoke as she approached.

'What did you do that for?'

''Cos I want to talk to you.'

'What about?'

Fraser was still standing on the step waving goodbye to the disappearing bus.

'Not here. We'll go to my garden.'

She grabbed his arm and pulled him on the way. 'Come on.'

There was no denying it. The show went down a treat, and the old people loved it.

PJ, as master of ceremonies, was on top form, and though some of Duncan's tricks went a bit awry when Angel passed him the wrong prop at one point, nobody cared. Debbie and Tessa didn't put a foot wrong, and remembered their teeth and smiles all the way through their tap dance routine. Marcus and Amanda got lots of laughs, and the final sing-song led by Charlie, accompanied by Danny at the piano, nearly shook the rafters.

Mary's comment to Nicola and Charlie for organising the event, was all the praise they needed.

'Well done, my loves. I'm proper proud of you both.'

What she then went on to say was a bit of a surprise.

'What a shame Mr Doyle wasn't here. He'd have loved it.'

It was Nicola who asked the question.

'Who's Mr Doyle?'

'Used to be one of our regulars, but he's housebound now, poor soul. Still I'll talk to you about him another time.'

And with that she was on her way back to her friend, Mrs Haggerty, who she'd been sitting with, and pointing out and praising her grandchildren, much to Mrs Haggerty's disgruntlement.

Debbie had had a niggle of worry all the way through the entertainment, and at one point had said as much to Nicola.

'I wish our Jemma'd come. I don't like to think of her being alone with that creep Lee.'

Nicola had been fairly relaxed about it.

'She'll be all right. You know our Jem.'

'That's the problem.'

If Debbie had heard Jemma and Lee's conversation in their garden she might have been even more worried.

They sat side by side on the bench as Jemma got the conversation underway.

'So tell me the real reason you went begging.'

'What you so keen to know for?'

'I just am. So go on.'

'All right. Only don't tell no one, mind? I don't want it getting back to that lot.'

'Cross me heart and hope to die.'

'Me dad was made redundant, see? It ain't easy keeping us all on what he gets on social.'

'How many are there?'

'There's three little 'uns as well as me.'

Jemma was taking it in avidly.

'What about your mam?'

'She was killed in an accident.'

'Oh Lee. That's awful.'

'We manage. The begging money helped buy the kids things. Me dad thought I had a paper round, right?'

'So why didn't you?'

'Made more money begging.'

'Well I think you're very brave. I couldn't do it.'

'You wouldn't have to, would you? You've got a proper family.'

And Lee having been honest with her, Jemma decided to share her big secret with him.

'If I tell you something, will you promise to keep it a secret?'

Lee gave a curt nod of agreement.

'It's about me mam . . .'

And the last of the Dobson daughters proved that she too was no great secret-keeper.

As soon as the last song was underway Debbie found Nicola.

'Has she turned up?'

'No sign yet.'

Then she went straight to Tessa who still hadn't changed back into her street clothes.

'Right, Tessa man, hurry up.'

'What's the rush?'

'I want to get back and find our Jemma.'

'Stop worrying. Besides I'm waiting for Geoff and the bus. I'm too shattered to walk.'

'I'll see you there.'

And with that Debbie was off.

She ran all the way, and arrived back at the Grove, exhausted. As she went up the path to the main door, she saw a figure in the distance, bending over Speedy's bike; then she was inside calling for Jemma, but no reply was forthcoming.

In the bus on the way back a sing-song was soon started up, and Geoff, sitting next to Alison, was quietly chuffed.

'I've got to hand it to them this time. They certainly did us proud.'

Alison was equally pleased.

'Yes, they're a smashing bunch. Makes it all the more of a shame that . . . '

But she left it unsaid.

Geoff looked around to make sure he wasn't in danger of being overheard before he spoke.

'Might be some news there.'

'Good?'

'Ian thinks they've got us premises.'

'Where?'

'He'll have all the gen on Monday. So fingers crossed, eh?'

'It won't be another Byker Grove.'

'Might be even better.'

Alison gave her most beaming smile.

'You're just a great big, cock-eyed optimist, Mr Keegan.'

'How else could I do this job?'

Spuggie and Marcus were sitting side by side happily chatting about chess, and in the seat behind them, sitting by herself,

Amanda was watching them, not knowing that Tessa was watching her, also from the seat behind.

Finally Tessa leant forward and whispered to her. 'Maybe he doesn't try so hard.'

Amanda spun round to see who spoke.

'What?'

'I said, your brother. Maybe he's making friends because he doesn't try so hard.'

Amanda was furious that someone who had been so rude in rejecting a friendly gesture earlier, should say such a thing to her.

'And what would you know about making friends?'

Tessa just gave a shrug and sat back again.


Spuggie's raucous voice cut through the chorus that was being sung like a buzz-saw.

'I'm starving. Are we all going for chips when we get back?'

And everybody shouted their agreement.

Winston, hearing Speedy's voice also agreeing, stood up and pointed.

'We are; he's not.'

Speedy looked around to see who Winston was talking about.

'Who's not?'

'You're not. Early night for you, sunshine, we want you fighting fit for tomorrow.'

Then Winston loudly chanted:

'Don't be late, Speedy's great, he'll win the cup for Byker!'

And they all finally took up the chant, and a blushing Speedy decided that losing a bag of chips was a very small price to pay for such fame.


Not having found Jemma in the club, Debbie came and stood on the doorstep, just in time to see Lee approaching. She called to him.

'Where's our Jemma?'

'How the heck should I know?'

'She stopped here with you.'

'That was hours ago. She pushed off somewhere.'

'Where?'

'Give us a break! I'm not her keeper.' And slowly his face changed, his lips lifted, and his eyes shone, the glower left his face. And something about his cold and cruel smile chilled her through to the heart, and she knew he was somehow responsible for the fact that she hadn't found Jemma inside the building.

# CHAPTER THREE

The day of the race dawned bright and clear, and as Speedy worked in his bedroom, through the group of exercises that Winston had given him, Spuggie, as promised, organised breakfast.

Winston, who had popped in to check that Speedy was on top form before going to join Debbie and Kelly in a pre-race 'money for the memorial' car wash, stood in the kitchen and watched in amazement as Spuggie, humming happily to herself, sorted the breakfast tray.

'That for Mr Wonderful?'

Spuggie looked at the spread happily.

'I squeezed the orange juice myself.'

'What's that on his cornflakes? Bird seed?'

'Wheatgerm. Lou says it's good for you. And honey on his toast, that's for energy. Hang on ...' She crossed to the flower vase and took a bloom that was only wilting slightly and then went back to lay it on the tray. 'There. Done.'

Winston couldn't understand it.

'Why aren't you moaning and groaning like you usually do?'

'Why should I? Speedy's my friend.'

'Well, he's my friend as well but I wouldn't sort his breakfast out and give him a blimmin' flower.'

'He doesn't enter for cycle races every day, does he?'

Winston had seen enough and was ready for the off.

'Ah well. Keep up the good work, kid. I'm off.'

'Why? Where you going?'

'Bit of business to attend to.'

'What about the race?'

'I'll be back in plenty of time.'

Heading for the door, Winston helped himself to a piece of toast off the tray in passing, and Spuggie was about to protest noisily, when a yell of agony from Speedy's room stopped them both in their tracks, and sent them running in that direction.

They found Speedy lying on the floor writhing in agony and rubbing his left calf.

Instantly reading the signs, Winston dashed to take over the massaging, as Speedy made his protest.

'It's all those rubbish exercises you gave me to do.'

'They weren't rubbish, they were isometric. Meant to make your calf muscles stronger.'

'They're very strong now, aren't they? They're tied up in reef knots.'

It was Spuggie who shut their shouting up.

'Calm down, lads. It's just cramp. It'll pass. I'll make you both a nice hot cup of tea, how's that?'

As she went off humming quietly to herself, both Winston and Speedy watched her disappearing back, bemused at her niceness. Winston had a thought.

'Has she had a personality transplant, you reckon?'

Speedy simply shook his head, baffled.


In the posh street where they'd arranged to meet Winston, stood Kelly and Debbie with their buckets and cloths waiting impatiently. It was Debbie who said it for both of them.

'Typical. He tells us to be here then he doesn't bother to turn up himself.'

Kelly was just giving her thought, 'He's probably still snoring,' when she saw trouble approaching behind Debbie's back.

It was the same Denton Burn boys who had harassed them the day before, Greg leading the way once more.

Debbie saw the look on Kelly's face and turned to stare in that direction.

As he approached, Greg spoke sarcastically.

'Well, well. And who's a naughty pair of little girls then, not doing what they were told?'

Kelly wasn't intent on showing her fear.

'It's a free country. There's no law that says we can't clean cars here.'

Greg walked right up to her and put his face menacingly close to hers.

'Yes, there is, Denton Burn's law.'

Debbie tugged at Kelly's shoulder.

'Come on, let's go.'

But Kelly was adamant.

'No, we won't. We don't have to do what they say.'

Greg moved even closer, and his voice carried real threat.

'I'm getting tired of your lip, kiddo. Now are you going to hoppit or are we going to make you?'

At that point a smaller boy had seen enough.

'Leave her alone, Greg.'

Greg turned and grinned at him.

'Nah, she's cheeky this one, Noddy.'

With that he turned back and took Kelly's glasses before she could manage to stop him.

'I don't like little girls who don't do what they're told.'

Kelly started tussling with him trying to get her glasses back, and Debbie, who by then was really getting frightened, called to her.

'Leave it, Kelly. Come on.'

But Kelly carried on struggling with him.

'I'm not scared of bullies.'

As Debbie ran to the end of the road hoping to find help, Greg laughed meanly at Kelly's remark.

'That right, Kelly-belly?'

And Kelly, even though she was frightened, still stood her ground.

Once more the boy called Noddy spoke.

'Let her go, Greg man. She's only a girl.'

Now Greg's anger was directed at him.

'Butt out, Noddy. I think young Kelly-belly here wants teaching a lesson, eh lads?' He glanced round the rest of the group looking for agreement and their smiling reaction gave him it.

At the end of the road Debbie was relieved to see Winston approaching.

'Winston! You've got to help!'

Sensing the urgency Winston ran to where she stood at the corner and looked down the street. He saw Kelly surrounded by the boys. With only the slightest hesitation he was on his way, and in seconds was facing Greg.

'That's enough. Let her go. If you've a fight with anyone it's with me. It was my idea.'

Again the sneer was in Greg's voice.

'That right? Well, don't have any more bright ideas, squirt, it's bad for your health.'

He turned back to Kelly.

'All right, scarper. That goes for the lot of you. And don't let us see you on our patch again, got it?'

Winston reached over and took Kelly's glasses from Greg's hand, and then with all the dignity they could muster he and Kelly went to join Debbie on the corner. All the boys laughed except Noddy, who watched them go, not happy about the incident.


The starting point for the cycle race was thronged with people. Not only cyclists but supporters from all over the North were milling about waiting for the off.

Jemma and Angel, having got there early, had found a terrific seat, a wall only metres from the start, and Jemma was having great fun harassing Speedy's opposition.

'There's that Terry Cowgill from Denton Burn. Yah! You've got no chance!'

But Angel was a bit bemused.

'What've we come so early for? Nobody else is hardly here yet.'

'Get a good view.'

But Angel wasn't fooled.

'You want to see that beggar boy again, don't you?'

'He's not a beggar boy!'

'He's revolting whatever he is.'

'You don't know anything about him.'

'Neither do you.'

'That's where you are wrong, clever clogs, I know a lot about him.'

'Like what?'

'His business.'

'Means you don't know.'

'He doesn't want it blabbing to silly little kids like you.'

Angel hardly had time to get a sulk underway when she saw Speedy approaching, with Spuggie pushing his bike. She pointed him out to Jemma.

'Look! Speedy's limping.'

Jemma bawled in that direction.

'I hope you're going to win, Speedy, man, I've got all my pocket money on you.'

And Spuggie called back cheerily:

'Of course he's going to win.'

But Angel asked the obvious.

'Why's he limping then?'

Again Spuggie answered on his behalf.

'He just had a bit of cramp but it doesn't hurt now.'

Speedy was suitably irate.

'Oh doesn't it? Like whose leg is it anyway?'

But Spuggie made her next comment to Angel and Jemma benevolently.

'Pre-race nerves.'

Seeing Marcus in the distance she called out:

'Hi, Marcus!' And passing the bike to Speedy went off to talk to him.

At that moment Jemma saw Lee drifting through the throng.

'Hey, Lee! You can come and sit with us if you like!'

Angel hissed it at her. 'Why can he?'

'Because I say so. Hutch up.'

Angel begrudgingly made room on the wall, as Lee climbed up, settled down and got a sweet packet out of his pocket, announcing the contents as he did so.

'Chocolate caramel.'

Angel said it as a quiet mutter.

'I bet they're poisoned.'

But took one nonetheless.

Spuggie, arriving at Marcus's side, was a bit lost as to what to say, so kept on safe ground.

'Where's your sister?'

'She didn't want to come. She thinks nobody likes her.'

'Nobody liked me when I first started coming.'

He looked at her intently.

'How long did that last?'

'A lot of them still don't. Doesn't bother me.'

He smiled.

'I think you're okay, Spuggie.'

Spuggie felt herself blush, she wasn't used to compliments.

'Do you?'

Marcus grinned as he said it.

'Any girl who can play chess like you can, can't be all bad.'

And Spuggie was absolutely thrilled.

Now the Grovers were gathering with a vengeance. A little distanced from Spuggie and Marcus, Charlie and Nicola were deep in a serious discussion. Before they'd left the house, Mary had asked them to consider visiting Mr Doyle occasionally.

'I don't know, Nic, he might resent us barging in.'

'And he might be grateful. You heard what Gran said, he's totally housebound.'

'Why's it down to us though? We don't even know him.'

'That's what everyone always says. "It's nothing to do with us, leave it to someone else".'

Charlie gave up the uneven struggle.

'All right, Mother Teresa. If it'll shut you up, I'll come.'

PJ and Danny were also near the starting point. PJ spoke his thought intently.

'Speedy better come in first, man.'

Danny looked at him and nodded his agreement.

'He certainly better. I've got two quid riding on him.'

But PJ had other things on his mind.

'It's more than that. A Byker Grove win would be brilliant publicity in our fight.'

Danny shook his head.

'Get real, PJ, we haven't got a fight. If the council say they're going to sell, they'll sell. We can't do 'owt about it . . .'

Danny stopped talking as he noted a girl in the crowd.

'What is it?' PJ asked.

Danny continued to stare at her. The last time he'd seen her it was on the tow path and she was being attacked by a lout.

'I know that girl.'

PJ glanced at her and gave a smile.

'Very fit.'

Danny shook his head.

'She's trouble, man.'

The girl in question had moved to join Tessa who was now standing talking with Charlie and Nicola.

'Hiya, Tess. What you doing here?'

Tessa looked up and seeing who it was, smiled.

'Supporting Byker Grove. Chrissie, this is Nicola and Charlie. Chrissie's in my school.'

Nicola, recognising her, started to say it before she could stop herself.

'Aren't you the girl who . . . ?'

But then didn't quite know what to say.

Chrissie smiled.

'Aren't I the girl who . . . what?'

Nicola took a quick glance at Charlie and her nod confirmed it.

'Nothing.'

Tessa got the conversation moving again, asking the big question of the day.

'Who you supporting?'

'Nobody special.'

And then Chrissie gave a smile.

'I'm just here to see all those gorgeous sexy male legs!'

As she moved off, Nicola made her comment to Charlie.

'She'll get into hot water if she doesn't watch it.'

Charlie agreed.

'Do you think we should tell her about the self-defence class that Alison is organising for us all?'

'Be no point. She wouldn't listen. I know the type.'

And Charlie had to agree once more.

As Winston, Kelly and Debbie arrived, Speedy, who had been watching out for Winston, crossed in that direction.

'At last, man. Where the heck you been?'

'Little hitch. Sorry.'

'Leave him alone, Speedy – he's been saving my life,' said Kelly.

Winston played it down. 'I didn't do nothing.'

Debbie said it for her.

'You did. You were brilliant.'

As Kelly and Debbie moved off to join the rest of the girls, Winston pointed at Speedy's calf.

'How's the leg now?'

'Okay. But I'm not favourite any more. He is.'

He nodded at Terry Cowgill who was doing a few nonchalant knee bends as a last minute limbering up. Winston was perplexed.

'Why?'

'Dunno. Marcus is the bookie, ask him.'

At that moment, Lee, having noticed Speedy's limp was just trying to get Marcus to accept another fiver which he turned down.

'Just one more quid then.'

'I can't give you the same odds I did before. He's down to three to one now.'

'Yeah. All right then.'

Marcus was just jotting the bet down in a note book, as Geoff and Fraser arrived at the far side.

Geoff couldn't quite make out what was going on.

'What's that new lad up to?'

By the time Fraser looked Marcus had popped the book back into his pocket again.

'What?'

Geoff decided to let it go.

'Nothing.'

And with that the organisers were calling the riders to the start. In no time, to the accompaniment of excited shouting from everybody, particularly the group from Byker Grove who couldn't stop screaming their encouragement to Speedy, the race was underway. The bystanders, as if also taking their cue from the starting pistol, were running after the cyclists and shouting them down the street.

Jemma and Angel were bawling at the top of their voices: 'We are the champions! We are the champions!'

And seeing that Lee wasn't joining in, Jemma egged him on to doing so. 'Come on, Lee, join in.'

Lee gave his smile.

'Yeah, all right.' And then half-heartedly shouted it.

'May the best man win.'

As the bikes disappeared from view, the crowd slowed to a walk and Danny found himself standing next to Tessa and the girl from the tow path. She smiled at him.

'Well, if it isn't the milk boy.'

Tessa was interested.

'You know each other?'

Danny for once couldn't bring himself to be sociable and simply said sourly, 'We've met,' before walking off.

Chrissie watched him go.

'Touchy, isn't he?'

And Tessa said, with surprise in her voice, 'Not usually.'

Speedy managed to stay in the lead the whole way, and was thrilled with the excitement of it, then he faced a final hill. He knew he only had to go over the top and down the far side, then at the bottom, turn right, and go a few hundred metres along the final straight which would take him back to the starting point, which was now the finishing line. There the throng would be waiting to greet them, and what a greeting he would get if he won. Speedy strained to get to the top of what soon became an endless hill, knowing that if he made it to the top first, chances are nobody would be able to catch up with him. By now he ached in every muscle, but it was a good ache, as his feet pushed down driving him and his bicycle ever onwards and upwards. The hot sun was burning down on him from a peerless blue sky as he saw the brow of the hill was in striking distance.

He counted out twenty downward pushes with each leg using the last vestige of his strength, and the final number, twenty, had him sweeping to the top of the hill, breasting it, and heading down the other side. And suddenly he was struck with horror. He had already dreamt of this moment and it had ended in disaster. He tried to put the niggling worry from his mind, as he started to gather speed and the sheer exhilaration of free-wheeling started to take over.

But then once more he remembered his dream, and fear touched him again.

He was moving at ever increasing speed. He realised that soon he would have to brake just to prove they worked, but put it off for as long as he dared, just thrilling to the immense speed he was managing. He put the moment off, and put it off, but finally he could put it off no more, and applied the brakes gently. The dream had been right! Nothing happened. More pressure. Still nothing. Then he jammed them full on. The bicycle simply increased its speed. He was hurtling down like a bullet.

The road below flattened and then quickly curved away to the right and he could see the crowd gathered there for the finish, but there was no way he could manage to take the curve at the speed he was travelling.

For the second time he was going to hit the pavement! And then he hit it with a sickening wheel-buckling thud; and he was off the bike and flying, his hands stretched out in front of him as if to ward off the tree that was directly in his flight path, but it was no good, it didn't move.

He was going to hit the tree head on! He ducked his head to one side, and felt his shoulder take the weight of the blow as everything went black.

The Byker bunch were running for the spot where Speedy had crashed as Terry Cowgill swept past and onwards to the winning post. Speedy was amazed to discover he was still conscious even though his shoulder was giving him agony, and he realised if it hadn't been for his dream it would have been his head that took the brunt, probably with dire consequences. Winston arrived running to his side, neck and neck with Geoff.

'What the heck happened, man?'

Speedy nodded his head bemused.

'I don't know, brakes just went.'

Winston almost screamed it at him.

'I told you, you should have taken it to a proper shop! I told you!'

Geoff eased him to one side.

'Not just now, Winston!'

He went to kneel where Speedy lay.

'Let's have a look at you, lad. No bones broken, can you get up, son?'

Speedy sat up with effort. His shoulder was bruised, his ankle all swollen and he was bleeding a bit from some scratches where his face had scraped past the tree, but otherwise he was okay.

Towards the back of the crowd Jemma said it to Lee quietly.

'Poor old Speedy. What a horrible thing to happen.'

Lee smiled, and then quickly wiped it away.

'Yeah. Shocking.'

Jemma, seeing the smile, wondered why.

At the Grove grounds, Kelly and Debbie walked up the path with a depressed and thoughtful Winston.

'Don't worry, Win. Speedy'll be okay.'

Debbie agreed.

'Yeah. Geoff's taken him to Casualty. They'll fix him up.'

Winston came out of his reverie.

'Who? Oh – Speedy, right.'

Debbie was surprised.

'Isn't that what you're looking so miserable about?'

'No.'

Kelly thought she had the answer.

'It doesn't matter that Denton Burn won – it's only a race.'

Winston stopped and looked at them.

'We didn't just lose the race, we lost our dosh as well.'

Kelly was aghast.

'You bet it, didn't you?! Gill's memorial money. You bet it all on Speedy!'

Winston spat it out. 'Yeah, that thicko.'

Debbie sprang to his defence.

'It wasn't his fault his brakes failed.'

'Well whose fault was it then?'

And at that Debbie remembered how the day before she had seen a figure at Speedy's bike. And as she played the scene over again in her mind, she realised with a shock of absolute horror, who it had been, and what he must have been doing.

Off in one corner of the grounds Marcus was working out the odds, as Spuggie, acting as banker, paid out the winners.

Spuggie saw Lee arrive and looked at Marcus questioningly.

Marcus glanced at Lee and nodded his head.

'Yeah. Give him fifty.'

'Pence?'

Lee sneered. 'Pounds.'

Spuggie was amazed.

'How much?!'

But Lee was speaking to Marcus.

'It's sixty, with my original ten quid stake back. Plus another four for the pound I had on this morning.'

Marcus nodded to Spuggie.

'Make it sixty-four.'

Lee took the money from her, and went without a thank you.

Spuggie watched him go as she spoke.

'I bet I know where he got that ten quid from and all.'

Marcus looked at her sharply.

'Nicked it?'

Spuggie shook her head in disgust.

'Telling lies about being starving! Slimeball.'

But Lee couldn't care less what Spuggie thought of him. He had other things on his mind. He went to join Angel and Jemma, where they sat by the slide.

'Right, girls. Burger and chips, milkshakes, whatever you want. My treat.'

Jemma was thrilled.

'Brilliant.'

Then remembered his dad and his brothers and sister.

'Shouldn't you save it to give to you know . . .' She cupped her mouth with her hand and mouthed it so Angel wouldn't hear, '. . . them?'

He smiled.

'There'll be plenty left. You coming or what?'

Jemma had no hesitation.

'Yeah. Come on, Ange.'

And even though Angel was reluctant, she still joined them so as not to be left alone.

Debbie having already watched Marcus and Spuggie paying Lee his winnings, now watched Jemma and Angel going down the path to the front gate with him, and by the time they had gone through the gate, she had come to a definite conclusion, but the question was what to do about it?

Slowly the afternoon drifted away, and all the gang drifted away with it, and the Grove was soon deserted except for a morose Winston who, lost in his thoughts, swung gently on a swing. Geoff saw him sitting there as he drove into the grounds, with the bits of Speedy's bike in a heap on the car roof. Geoff slowed the car to a halt, and called out:

'Don't worry, he'll live.'

Coming out his reverie Winston looked up and saw it was Geoff.

'Who?'

'Speedy. I've just dropped him home.'

Without looking Geoff stretched his hand out the window to point at the wreck on the roof.

'Don't know about this though. I'm taking it to the shop tomorrow, but I don't give a lot for its chances.'

'I told him he should have it overhauled proper. Wally.'

Geoff got out of the car and then crossed to Winston as he spoke accusingly.

'He *hurt* himself, man. What's bugging you?'

Winston was bitter.

'Only dropped the rotten lot, didn't I?'

Geoff waited till he was level with Winston before speaking.
'I'm not with you?'

'Every penny we made for Gill's memorial! Down the pan.'

There was cool moment of contemplation before Geoff said, very quietly, 'I think you had better come inside.'

And as Geoff set off for the Grove, too late Winston realised he had blown it.

PJ had talked Danny into going to the ice rink, and now as Danny tied his boot laces up he wasn't too happy.

'I don't know what the heck I let you talk me into this for, PJ.'

PJ had the answer ready.

'Be a laugh. Soon have you whirling around on that ice, man.'

Danny having finally got the boots on, tried standing on the edge of the ice and immediately went flying.

'I can't even walk, let alone whirl!'

But PJ wasn't looking at him. He was more interested in Chrissie on the other side of the rink.

'She can though. Look at her go.'

Chrissie was doing an amazing pirouette on the spot. Danny lifted himself to his feet, clinging to the rail as he looked in her direction.

'Show off.'

Tessa arriving at their side with a whoosh of splaying ice, heard Danny's remark and guessed who it was aimed at.

'She isn't. She's just good at it, she's been doing it for years.'

Chrissie was also crossing in their direction, and arriving addressed her remark at Danny:

'Come on then if you're coming.'

And as Danny bravely stepped on to the rink once more, she grabbed his hands and turning her back to him, put them on her waist.

'Hold on to me.'

And as he did so, she was off, and like it or not Danny was following behind desperately hanging on.

Round about the same time that Danny was making an undignified circuit of the ice rink, clinging on to a laughing

Chrissie as best he could, Nicola and Charlie were approaching a shabby house in one of Newcastle's rougher streets. They noted, as they walked up the path to the door, that the garden on either side of the pathway was weedy and unkempt.

Charlie spoke it in a whisper.

'Are you sure this is it?'

Nicola checked the number on the paper her gran had given her, and then rang the doorbell as she spoke.

'Yes. Twenty-eight.'

Charlie looked at the windows.

'The curtains are all drawn, perhaps he's out.'

Nicola shook her head.

'He never goes out any more. That's the whole point.'

Again she rang the bell as she spoke and still there was no response.

Charlie had a sudden worry.

'He's probably asleep. He won't thank us for disturbing him. Come on, Nicola – let's go.'

Charlie turned to go as Nicola tried ringing the bell one last time, but they were both stopped in their tracks, as a bolt was drawn, the door creaked open, and the face of a cross-looking old man appeared from behind the door's chain.

'All right, all right! I'm not deaf! What do you want?'

It was Nicola who asked the obvious.

'Mr Doyle?'

'I'm not buying anything,' came the curt reply.

Charlie smiled her sweetest smile.

'We're not selling anything, Mr Doyle.'

But it was totally wasted on him.

'So what you bothering me for then?'

Nicola exchanged a glance with Charlie. This was proving tougher than expected.

'We didn't mean to disturb you. My gran thought you might like a visit. She's Mrs O'Malley.'

'Never heard of her.'

Charlie took over.

'Mary O'Malley. She goes to the Day Centre.'

'Lot of nattering old biddies there, no sense between the lot of them.'

At that he removed the chain, and opened the door, and both thought that with a bit of luck he was going to tell them to go away. But it was the opposite.

'I suppose you best come in. Mary O'Malley? Is she the skinny one with no teeth?'

Nicola was appalled. 'No, she's not!'

But he was off into the darkness beyond expecting them to follow.

Charlie said what Nicola was thinking.

'I thought she said he was a sweet old thing?'


Geoff was in the office, chatting on the telephone to Ian Mc-Dowell about the place he had on offer as a substitute for the club's headquarters.

'Obviously I don't expect it to be the same; you only get a Byker Grove once in a lifetime. So long as it's got possibilities.'

But seeing Marcus and Spuggie passing the door he cupped the phone and yelled at them:

'You two! A word!'

Then once more into the phone.

'Right, Ian mate, I'll look into it. And thanks.'

And having put the telephone down he was ready to deal with Spuggie and Marcus.

'So. What's this I've been hearing?'

Marcus was the soul of innocent charm.

'What about, sir?'

'You running a book on the cycle race.'

'Ah.'

'Yes indeed "Ah". I suppose you know all forms of gambling are strictly barred here?'

Spuggie butted in before Marcus could foolishly admit it.

'No, he didn't. He's new.'

Geoff wasn't having it.

'You're not, Spuggie. You know the rules better than anyone.'

And then it was Marcus's turn to leap to her defence.

'She had nothing to do with it, it was all my idea.'

'Well, it wasn't a very bright idea, sunshine. In fact it was a downright rotten idea. And I suggest you don't get any of those ideas again, not if you want to keep on coming here. That clear?'

'Yes, sir. Sir?'

'Well?'

'Are you going to tell my father?'

Geoff shook his head.

'We don't usually snitch to parents unless we meet continual non-cooperation.'

He noted the look of relief in Marcus's face.

'Blow his top, would he?'

'Something like that.'

'All the more reason to watch it then, eh? Right, clear off.'

Geoff shook his head wryly as they went.

'Kids!'


In Mr Doyle's living room, as instructed Nicola and Charlie sat on the sofa, and faced him where he sat in a straight-backed wooden chair staring at them. To one side a very old and moth-eaten parrot in a cage also kept a beady eye on them.

After a while Mr Doyle broke the silence.

'If it's money you're after I've got none.'

Nicola said it for both of them.

'We're not after your money, Mr Doyle . . .'

'That's good, 'cos I've got none.'

And then what she had called him finally sunk in.

'And no "mister". I've never been mister. I was bosun once. Now it's just Doyle.'

Charlie chipped in, glad to air her knowledge.

'Bosun? Were you in the Navy?'

'Merchant ships, aye. Two world wars. Saw the lot.'

Again silence fell, and stayed fallen, until Nicola tried to lift it with an explanation.

'The thing is, my gran, Mrs O'Malley, she thought you might like us to visit you from time to time.'

He was bemused.

'What for?'

And Charlie, though she would have thought it was obvious, said:

'Well, for company.'

Mr Doyle nodded at the moth-eaten parrot who nodded back.

'Got Nelson there. Don't need nobody else.'

'Good old Nelson,' echoed the parrot.

Nicola thought desperately for something they could do.

'Perhaps we could tidy round for you.'

'You're touching nothing! I'm not having me things messed about.'

Charlie added her thought.

'What about shopping?'

'What about it?'

'Charlie means we could do some for you.'

'Charlie? That's a lad's name.'

Charlie explained. 'It's a nickname really. I'm Marilyn Charlton but everybody calls me Charlie.'

'I shall call you Marilyn.'

He turned to glower at Nicola.

'And you, what do they call you?'

'Nicola.'

'Another fancy name. King Edwards.'

Charlie and Nicola exchanged a bemused glance then Nicola asked the question for both of them.

'What?'

'Spuds. Five pounds. And a brown loaf, sliced, and don't let them fob you off with stale. Did you say you'd do me shopping for me or not?'

Nicola and Charlie spoke it together.

'Er yes. Of course we will.'

With which he got out a small leather purse and started counting money out, grumbling on as he did so.

'And think on. I want the proper change fetching back. Just because I'm old doesn't mean I'm senile.'

Debbie had popped into the Metro Centre for a look round, and seeing nothing and nobody that caught her fancy was making her way home when she saw Lee on the other side of the street. She crossed to him calling as she did so.

'I want to talk to you.'

He stood and waited for her to arrive.

'Oh yes?'

'You're to keep away from our Jemma.'

His eyes hooded slightly.

'Who says so?'

'Me. And if you don't I'll tell her what you did.'

He continued to eye her coldly.

'And what's that, Miss Know-all?'

Debbie took a deep, courage-inducing breath, before letting him have it.

'You fixed Speedy's bike.'

She had expected him to look frightened, but he didn't, simply smiled.

'Why would I do that?'

''Cos you bet on Terry Cowgill. I saw Marcus giving you your winnings.'

The smile went.

*Good* she thought, *that's knocked the smirk from his lips.*

For the first time there was an edge of the defensive in his voice.

'Proves nothing. Loads of kids did.'

'And I saw you mucking about with Speedy's bike yesterday.'

'You see a lot of things, don't you?'

'I'm not stupid.'

And then, frighteningly, his face moved close, and she saw his eyes were burning into hers.

'I hope you're not. 'Cos I tell you that would be stupid. To go blabbing to your kid sister or anybody else.'

'Why shouldn't I?'

'Because I've got certain powers.'

'What powers?'

His voice was now coming in a terrifying whisper.

'I can do things. Make things happen. I can wish bad luck on people.'

Debbie tried to fight her fear and failed.

'I don't believe you.'

He continued just as quietly threatening.

'Some call it the Evil Eye. I just think of it as a gift. There was this cat kept scratching me.' He miaowed loudly, straight into her face and made her jump with the shock of it, then carried on talking as if he hadn't done it. 'I put the hex on it, next thing it was all stretched out only fit for a moggy rug.'

Debbie tried to get back in control with sarcasm.

'You've seen too many horror pictures, you have.'

'Yeah. Scary, aren't they.'

'They don't scare me. They're only make-believe.'

He smiled at her icily.

'Hang on to that thought, kid.'

His final stare didn't shift, just went on and on and she found she couldn't take her eyes from his. Debbie was suddenly really terrified and still the stare continued. Then finally with a bark of a laugh he turned away and ran cackling up the road. She was watching him go, aghast, when suddenly a hand touched her shoulder. She screamed out loud, and turned as she called it.

'Leave us alone, pig!'

It was the boy from Denton Burn, Noddy.

'I only wanted to speak to you.'

Realising who it was Debbie was suspicious.

'What about?'

'Aren't you the girl who was washing cars?'

'So?'

'Where can I find your mates?'

And, taken by surprise, Debbie told him.

In the general room, Tessa, who was showing Chrissie around, introduced her to Kelly and Winston in passing.

'This is Kelly; and that one's Winston.'

They all exchanged greetings, as Tessa continued.

'Chrissie's thinking of joining here.'

Kelly smiled.

'It's ace, you'll like it.'

At which Chrissie saw Danny and PJ entering.

'Will I like the people who come here though?'

As she looked in that direction, Danny also turned and saw her and spoke it under his breath for PJ's benefit.

'Oh no! Not Boedicea again. What's she doing here?'

But PJ was watching another stranger who had just arrived. Noddy.

Noddy went straight over to Winston and Kelly.

'Hello.'

Winston saw who it was.

'Oh, it's you. If they've sent you to warn us off again, you can tell 'em to get knotted.'

'They haven't, I came off me own bat.'

Kelly was surprised.

'What for?'

'I've left Denton Burn. Can't stand the place or the people. I want to come here.'

Kelly couldn't blame him.

'What do they call you?'

'Noddy.'

Winston was amazed.

'What?'

'Noddy.'

'Oh yeah, and I suppose your mate was Big Ears.'

Noddy laughed good-naturedly.

'That's good that is. Never heard that one before.'

Winston said it again, testing it.

'Noddy.'

Kelly thought he should lay off.

'Shut up, Winston.'

Noddy laughed.

'Winston? That's a pretty weird sort of name.'

'Not as weird as Noddy.'

But seeing who had also arrived at the door Winston had other things on his mind.

'Hey, Speedy, man! Come on in.'

And Speedy with one crutch, and his arm in a sling, hopped as best he could to the place where Winston organised a chair for him, and he was soon the centre of attention with all the Grovers gathering around to quiz him.

'They kept us in for a bit 'cos they thought I might have concussion.'

Angel, interested, asked for clarification.

'What's that?'

'When you're all confused and don't know where you are,' Tessa said.

Winston pretended to be bemused.

'How could they tell? He's like that anyway.'

At that Geoff entered and having greeted Speedy, called out for everyone's benefit.

'Just thought you'd like to know I'm off to look at the new premises. I don't suppose any of you'd like to come with me?'

And with that everybody screamed, 'Yes!' and headed for door, whooping with joy at the thought of it. Speedy left alone, called at Geoff's retreating back.

'What about me?'

Geoff called back:

'I'm sure they'll fetch you back a full report, my lad.'

As Geoff passed Fraser, who was staying behind to keep his eye on things, he asked after Spuggie.

'Where is she? She's another one who wouldn't want to miss out on this.'

'Gone off somewhere with that new boy.'

'Marcus? Is that a good idea?'

'He's only a bit stuck up. Spuggie'll soon bring him down to earth . . .'

But at that moment Marcus was making Spuggie see stars, millions of them.

Marcus's bedroom, she decided, was super flash. It doubled as an office/den and an observatory, with a large telescope by the window pointing to the sky. Spuggie asked her questions, awed.

'How many stars are there?'

'In our galaxy? About a hundred thousand.'

'How do you mean "our galaxy"?'

'There's billions of others.'

'Other worlds?'

'Going on and on into infinity.'

'I thought that was just in films. You know. "Close Encounters".'

'No, it's all out there. Planets, stars, quasars, nebulae, meteors.'

Spuggie was perplexed.

'How did it get there?'

'One theory is the Big Bang. A colossal primaeval explosion, and the galaxies are just the debris from it, still hurtling outwards through space for ever and ever.'

Spuggie stood by the telescope.

'And can you see all that through this?'

Before he could reply Amanda entered and spoke, at first not noticing that Spuggie was there. 'I'm writing to the Harringtons to see that Bonnie and Clyde are all . . .' At that she saw Spuggie, and Spuggie could sense she wasn't pleased. '. . . It's you.'

'I brought her to see my telescope.'

'Bore her to tears, you mean?'

But Spuggie wasn't having that.

'He's not. I think it's fantastic. Who's Bonnie and Clyde?'

Amanda said it quite sharply.

'Our dogs.'

'What kind?'

'Airedales.'

'They're nice. I like them.'

Amanda finally thawed a little.

'We had to leave them behind because of the quarantine rules.'

'That must have been horrible.'

'It was.'

Marcus smiled as he said it.

'She was besotted with those dogs, weren't you, Mand? Thought more of them than she does of me.'

Amanda also smiled.

''Course I did. They were more *intelligent* than you.'

Spuggie looked at Marcus.

'Are you coming back to the Grove?'

'I don't know.'

'You still upset over Geoff telling you off?'

Amanda was onto Spuggie's remark in a flash.

'What did he tell you off for, Marc?'

Spuggie, feeling quite guilty at dropping him in it, didn't speak.

'Marc? He found out, didn't he? I told you you were dumb doing that again.'

Spuggie's eyes widened at the revelation.

'Have you done it before?'

Marcus nodded.

'Only once. At school.'

And Amanda took up the story.

'Dad went berserk. He grounded Marcus for a month.'

'Is he dead strict then?'

Marcus said, drily, 'Let's just say we do what we're told.'

Amanda added equally drily, 'Usually.'

Spuggie decided to change the subject, but this time addressed both of them.

'Are you coming or what?'

Marcus and Amanda exchanged a glance, and Spuggie realised, pleased, that they'd decided to go.


'Nicola Dobson! You're not!'

'I am! I've got to, Charlie.'

Charlie was amazed that Nicola had decided she would go back and visit Doyle again.

'But why? Half an hour ago you said *never again.*'

'Yes, well, I've thought about it. We can't just abandon him even though he is an old misery. He's stuck on his own in that wretched little house, he can hardly hobble from one room to the next, we can't just give up because it's not *easy,* can we?'

Charlie got it in quick.

'What do you mean *we*?!'

But by then they were through the door and saw Speedy. Charlie's greeting cheered him up no end.

'Speedy! I didn't expect to see you! How are you?'

'Bit better, thanks.'

Nicola was also a bit surprised.

'What you doing here? Should you be out?'

'Lou brought us in the car. I got dead bored sitting at home.'

Charlie looked around.

'It's not exactly lively here, where is everyone?'

Fraser, passing through, gave the answer. 'Gone with Geoff to see the new premises. They should be back soon.'

Spuggie was coming through the door with Marcus and Amanda saying, 'Honest, it's dead good once you get to know everyone...' then saw the empty room. Fraser was a handy target for the question.

'Where are they all?'

'Giving the new place the once over.'

Spuggie was furious.

'They're not! Why the heck didn't they tell us?!'

Fraser shook his head in disbelief.

'Probably 'cos you weren't here.'

Spuggie almost stamped her foot with the fury of it.

'Typical!'

At which Jemma entered and asked Fraser the same question as Charlie and Spuggie, to which Fraser replied:

'I'm going to have a T-shirt printed saying, "They've all gone to look at the new premises".'

Spuggie added grimly:

'Without me.'

Jemma asked Spuggie: 'Has Lee gone with them?'

And Spuggie replied quite crossly, 'How should I know? I'm not there, am I?'

Speedy looked at Fraser.

'I see she's back to normal.'

Very soon afterwards Geoff and those who had been sightseeing with him, walked up to the Grove in silence, their faces saying it for them. Questions about the building flew from Spuggie,

Nicola, Charlie, Jemma and Speedy in a torrent and in return, all they got was monosyllabic misery.

'It's rubbish.'

'Zero.'

'Zilch.'

'I wouldn't keep pigs in it.'

'It's disgusting.'

'It's diabolical.'

'It's a mess.'

The silence that fell was broken by Jemma's tentative enquiry.

'So – it's no good then?'

And in spite of their sorrow, in the face of the question they had to laugh.

Nicola spoke through the laughter.

'The question is, what we going to do about it?'

And as silence fell once more, it was the new girl Chrissie who had the brilliant idea.

'Let's stage a demonstration round at the Town Hall, protesting at being forced out. We'll let them know we have a voice!'

Danny said it sulkily for PJ's benefit.

'And she's the one to do it.'

But PJ wasn't having that.

'Shut up, man! The girl's right.'

He called so all the Grovers present could hear.

'Do we let them walk all over us; just because we're kids?! Do we!'

In unison the call came back.

'No, we don't!'

And determined and angry, suddenly they were ready to do battle.

# CHAPTER FOUR

Breakfast at the Bewick household was always a strangely formal affair. Mr Bewick expected Amanda and Marcus to be dressed and ready for the day by the time they sat down, and conversation, while not being forbidden, was frowned on.

This morning Marcus didn't care. It really was something he had to have out with his father.

'Dad? I need to talk to you about Byker Grove.'

His father lowered his paper slightly, and looked at him coolly over the top of it, waiting for Marcus to continue.

'Can't you find another site to build your flats?'

Mr Bewick started reading his paper again as he spoke.

'You stick to your stars, son. This isn't your concern.'

Marcus was stung to reply.

'But they're my friends; they've got nowhere else decent to go.'

Mr Bewick flushed red, a thing that always happened when his children showed any spirit.

'I'm not prepared to discuss it. And I forbid you to interfere. Is that clearly understood?'

Marcus looked down at his plate, wondering if it was worth continuing. Then decided it wasn't.

'Yes, Dad.'

About the same time outside the bathroom at the Dobsons', Debbie finally got off her chest what she had been meaning to say to Jemma for days. In a word, that Lee was a ratbag, adding the thought that Jemma shouldn't have anything to do with him. Jemma of course was furious.

'I'll do what I want, you can't tell us what to do!'

'But he's awful, Jemma.'

'I think some of your friends are well gruesome, I don't tell you to stop going with 'em.'

Debbie jumped to her friends' defence.

'None of mine are like him.'

Jemma was honestly bemused.

'What's wrong with him?'

Debbie had no doubt.

'He's just no good.'

Jemma, knowing that Lee was motherless and was secretly helping to bring up three young children, answered furiously.

'Well, that's where you're wrong, see. Because I know things about him that you don't. Debbie stopped herself in time from blurting out the whole truth but simply hinted at it.

'And I know things about him that you don't.'

But Jemma had had enough, marching into the bathroom she closed the door behind her with a slam.

Everybody was going to be at the Grove after school to make placards but before going, Spuggie had some calls to make.

First she headed for the library.

Tessa was ahead in the queue and Spuggie called to her.

'What you doing here?'

'Same as you, I imagine.'

Then Tessa, having asked the librarian if there were any books on the history of Newcastle and been told, 'Shelvesful,' and having shouted 'See ya!' to Spuggie, set off in the direction indicated, and it was soon Spuggie's turn. Her request for a book about the stars led to the reply from the librarian.

'Pop or film?'

'No, I mean . . .'

'Horoscopes?'

'No.'

Spuggie didn't know what the word was.

'Like in the sky.'

'Astronomy. Last aisle on the left.'

Spuggie went off to the shelf and looked, and soon found the book that gave her the perfect excuse for visiting Marcus.

In the general room at the Grove, early birds at the placard-making stakes were busily at it, while at the piano Speedy and Danny tried to get a protest song underway.

Speedy thought, 'Byker Grove's body lies a mouldering in the grave . . .?' had a ring to it, but Danny thought it too negative.

'Sounds like we've already lost.'

He suggested his own version.

'Byker Grove's body is still putting up a fight...?'

Speedy smiled. 'Sounds like the title of horror film...'

Nearby Winston was putting the finishes to his placard.

### PRESTIGE PROPERTIES ARE MURDERERS

PJ viewed it with dismay.

'That's a bit strong, isn't it?'

'Losing your bottle, are you, PJ?'

PJ shook his head.

'No – but we won't get away with it.'

Angel, overhearing, chipped in.

'But it's true. They are killing the Grove between them.'

PJ caught sight of Angel's effort.

### COUNCIL CUTS ARE ADOMINABULL

'You don't spell "abominable" like that, Angel.'

She smiled at him sweetly. 'I do.'

Chrissie met Tessa coming from the library weighed down with
the chosen books in a carrier, and they set off to walk to Byker
Grove together. By the time they arrived and went through to
the general room, Danny and Speedy were belting out their
choice of song.

'We shall not be, we shall not be moved, we shall not be, we
shall not be moved...'

Chrissie called sarcastically to them.

'Oh, not that boring old dirge.'

Danny defended it.

'It's a right good protest song. What's wrong with it?'

'Can't you come up with something a bit more original?'

Speedy explained what was really going on.

'We're trying for new words to "John Brown's Body..."'

Crossing to the piano Chrissie said:

'Well – let's have a look then.'

She had just lifted the pad from the piano in front of Danny
when he grabbed it back, saying as he did so, 'This composing
team is Clark and Dimmoro.'

'I was only trying to help.'

Tessa, who had been watching, felt Danny was being unfair.

'She's only trying to help.'

'She can go and help with the placards then. Looks like they can do with it. Teach Angel how to spell for a start.'

As Chrissie and Tessa moved off, Speedy asked the question.

'What you got against her? Chrissie's all right.'

'I can't stand bossy women.'

Speedy looked to where she stood on the far side of the room.

'Well, I think she's pretty. Not as pretty as Charlie, though, but ... pretty.'

Just then, if Speedy had but known it, Charlie stood with Nicola on Doyle's doorstep as he stared in amazement at the bunch of flowers they both carried.

'What's them?'

They said it in harmony.

'Flowers.'

'I've no money to chuck away on flowers.'

Charlie held out the bunch as she spoke.

'Those are from us. We thought they'd cheer you up a bit.'

'Who said I needed cheering up?'

Ignoring the remark Nicola offered hers as well. Doyle looked at both bunches suspiciously before finally taking them.

'Should have waited a week or so. Save your spending for me funeral.'

And exchanging a glance, they followed him in.

Kath had insisted that Jemma and Debbie finish their homework before going to the Grove, and they had sat in the kitchen getting on with it, until a remark from Debbie got the morning's argument about whether Lee was a suitable friend or not underway once more, by hinting again that she knew something Jemma didn't.

Jemma decided she had the answer, and let it pour.

'You're just telling lies because you're jealous. You can't get a boyfriend of your own. You've been making up to PJ long enough and he won't take no notice of you.'

Debbie was now very angry.

'It's got nothing to do with PJ . . . '

And Jemma saw she'd found Debbie's weakness.

'Jealous cat, jealous cat, jealous . . . '

Luckily Kath arrived at that point.

'Debbie! Jemma! That's quite enough!'

Debbie got it in first.

'She was calling me names . . . '

And Jemma was a close second.

'She was bossing us about . . . !'

Kath interrupted before the row could get going again.

'You're both behaving like a pair of wild things. I won't have it. What kind of example is that going to set your new little brother or sister when it's born?'

Jemma stood and spat it out in fury.

'I don't care. I don't care what it does. I'm not having anything to do with it. I hate it!'

Kath said it surprisingly quietly considering.

'Don't say things like that, Jem. You don't mean them. And it's bad luck.'

Debbie was immediately all ears as Jemma shot off for the front door hiding her tears.

Kath called after her.

'You've got to finish your homework.'

And the call echoed back. 'Finished!'

Debbie was looking at her mother appraisingly.

'What do you mean, Mam – it's bad luck?'

'It's just wrong to talk about new babies like that.'

Debbie was suddenly frightened.

'You're going to be all right, Mam, aren't you? Say you are?'

Kath smiled. 'Of course I am, pet. What's brought this on?' And suddenly Debbie stood and was in Kath's arms wanting a cuddle just like she used to, before she had decided she was much too big for such foolishness.

'Mam? There's no such thing as the Evil Eye, is there?'

And Kath having assured her there wasn't, Debbie also set off for the Grove.

Doyle was dividing the flowers up between four empty milk bottles, still grumbling on that they should have waited a week till he died.

Nicola tried to stop the flow.

'Don't talk like that, Doyle. You'll be with us for a long time yet.'

Doyle shook his head dolefully.

'No, I shall go any day now. And about time too.'

Charlie was shocked.

'That's a terrible thing to say.'

He glanced at her sharply. 'And what would you know about it, miss? Here's me lingering on, of no use to neither man nor beast, with me legs conked out on me.'

Nicola smiled as she said it.

'We'll be your legs now, Doyle.'

But Doyle wasn't having her making light of his misery.

'I don't need pity.'

Charlie took the conversation over, trying to change the subject.

'We know you don't. We just want to help.'

Having finished with the flowers, Doyle wiped his hands on the back of his trousers to get rid of the leaves stuck to his palms.

'Right then. If you want to make yourselves useful, you can clean out Nelson's cage.'

Charlie and Nicola looked towards the wicked-looking parrot, aghast at the thought.

'Well, don't just stand there, he won't bite you. And if he does it'll only be a friendly nip, won't it, Nelson? Eh, boy?'

And the parrot nodded before saying it.

'Good old Nelson.'

While Debbie was making her way to the Grove she suddenly sensed she was being followed, she turned the corner and paused. Moments later Lee came round the corner furtively. He stopped when he saw her.

'Hiya.'

Debbie let him have her suspicions.

'Are you following me?'

He gave his irritating smile.

'Why would I do that?'

'Because you're weird, that's why.'

His smile had gone and he eyed her coldly.

'Just keeping an eye on you. We don't want anything bad to happen, do we?'

Though she said it bravely enough she didn't mean it. She was scared.

'You can't put spells on people, you're lying...'

'Am I?'

And with that he disappeared back round the corner again.

Debbie knew she was going to have to talk with someone soon. But who?

Spuggie arrived at Marcus and Amanda's home just as their father was getting into his car. As she passed him he looked at her coolly.

'Can I help you, young lady?'

Spuggie recognised him from his visit to the Grove.

'I'm a friend of Marcus's. Is he in?'

Mr Bewick switched the ignition on as he spoke.

'He's doing his homework. Don't keep him long, missy.'

Then as he drove off Spuggie went to ring the front doorbell. Marcus answered the ring and was equally cool.

'Yes?'

Spuggie desperately fought to find a reasonable excuse for being there apart from the book on stars, and then found it.

'I came to see if you're coming to help with the demo.'

He shook his head.

'I doubt it.'

Spuggie thought she knew why.

'I just saw your dad.'

'Nice for you. He needed some papers. Busy man. Like me.'

Spuggie decided not to take the hint.

'Going to ask us in then?'

'What for?'

'Could I see your telescope again?'

'I suppose so – just for a short while. And with that he moved aside to let her go ahead of him.

Marcus knew he would enjoy telling her more about the stars; how they were made of Hydrogen and Helium. How you couldn't land on them, like you could on Mars and the moon, because they were just gas and dust. How they shone because of their heat, and different colours meant different heats, white stars being hotter than red ones. He would enjoy telling her; but didn't yet realise that when she was near him, Spuggie saw stars without going anywhere near the telescope.

She didn't stay long – but by the time she left, she had decided it was time to sort herself out.


As Charlie and Nicola left Doyle's, Charlie asked the question.

'Does it hurt?'

Nicola stopped sucking the throbbing finger, where the parrot had bitten her, for a moment so she could answer.

'Only a bit. Vicious old thing.'

Charlie agreed.

'And the parrot's not so friendly either.'

Nicola smiled and went back to giving her finger a comforting suck, as the thought struck Charlie.

'I wonder if he's ever been married?'

'Who'd marry him?'

And Charlie had to agree that Nicola had a point.


At the Grove, sitting in his office with Alison, Geoff listened to the growing furore from the general room as the gang sang their campaign song ferociously to the tune of 'John Brown's Body.'

'Byker Grove Youth Club is the very best in town,
Byker Grove members say the council is a clown,
Byker Grove's body may be dead but won't lie down,
And its soul goes marching on!'

It was Alison who broke the silence that had fallen between them.

'They're certainly building up a fine head of steam out there.'

Geoff smiled at the understatement.

91

'Sounds like it.'

Alison voiced her worry.

'Puts you in an awkward position.'

Geoff looked at her.

'Not really. I just stay neutral.'

Alison shook her head in disbelief.

'It's hardly being neutral, when you know what they're planning.'

'You want me to step in and stop it?'

Alison knew Geoff knew that wasn't what she meant and said as much.

'You know perfectly well for two pins I'd grab one of those placards myself and march right up there alongside 'em.'

Geoff smiled.

'Exactly. Which is why I've suddenly come down with this acute attack of deafness and bad eyesight. Must be my age.'

Glancing through the window Alison saw that Spuggie was sitting in the grounds looking very downcast, and she decided she had better go and look into it.


Spuggie saw Alison approaching but didn't smile a greeting, just looked down again.

'Spuggie? Your mam's not bad again, is she?' Alison asked as she reached Spuggie.

Spuggie was surprised.

'No. Why?'

Alison sat down beside her.

'You look a bit miserable.'

Spuggie thought about it, and then looked at Alison intently.

'Can I ask you something?'

'It's what I'm here for, pet.'

It was a while before Spuggie could bring herself to say it.

'Do you think I'm ugly?'

Alison was shocked.

'Ugly? You? You've one of the bonniest little faces I've ever seen.'

'Yes, but would other people think that?'

At that Alison realised what the problem probably was.

'By other people, do I take it you mean boys?'

Spuggie hastily denied any such thing.

''Course not. I just hate all these freckles and red hair. Red hair's horrible.'

'No, it's not, it's gorgeous. The Duchess of York's got red hair, and she's not done so badly.'

Spuggie shook her head.

'I wish I looked like Charlie.'

'I bet Charlie sometimes wishes she looked like Spuggie.'

But Spuggie wasn't having it.

'You don't mean that. Nobody wishes she looked like us.'

And with that she was up and off for the entrance, leaving Alison sitting there quietly contemplating life, love, and its many twists and turns. And just for one brief and passing moment she remembered her own heartbreak, but shook her head quickly to remove the thought before it had chance to settle.

PJ was also intent on giving a counselling session. Having seen that Debbie was totally down and depressed about something he took her from the noisy general room, to the comparative quiet of the games room to give her a serious talking to.

'Debs, you've got tell us what's bugging you, because something is. Has been for days.'

Debbie's wide-eyed look said it even as she spoke.

'I'm scared, PJ...'

'What of?'

Debbie looked round the empty room as if expecting to be watched by someone.

'I can't...'

PJ knew he had to be forceful.

'Yes, you can, Debbie. What are you scared of? Have you been watching horror videos again?'

Debbie shook her head.

'No.'

'Then what?'

Debbie knew she must share it.

'It's him.'

PJ was perplexed.

'Who? Debs. Who is it? You've got to tell me.'

And finally Debbie did. And as she told the tale, PJ's lips got tight with anger, and he knew he must sort the matter out once and for all.


Charlie and Nicola were in the loo still talking about Doyle, and then Charlie wanted to know about Kath's baby, but Nicola preferred to change the subject, so was quite pleased when Spuggie arrived, stopping the private conversation dead.

Spuggie looked at Charlie's reflection in the mirror momentarily, then asked the question out of the blue.

'Is your hair natural?'

Charlie raised her eyebrows.

'Cheek, course it is.'

Undaunted by her reaction Spuggie persisted.

'But people can dye it that colour, can't they?'

Charlie shook her head.

'I haven't.'

'No, but I could.'

Nicola started washing her hands as she spoke.

'What the heck would you want to do that for?'

Spuggie shook her head sadly at her reflection in the mirror.

'I don't like the way I look.'

Charlie couldn't understand the problem.

'What's wrong with it?'

'I'm sick of it, my face, my stupid hair, my horrible clothes...'

Nicola spoke as she rinsed her hands and headed for the drier.

'Poor Spug. You are in a bad way.'

Spuggie went on staring at herself sadly.

'I've tried with make-up, but I always end up looking like Coco the Clown.'

Charlie and Nicola left Spuggie with her misery and went, and Spuggie just kept looking at herself in the mirror, depressed. Seconds later Charlie and Nicola popped their heads back in, and Nicola said:

'Hey, Spug. What are you doing straight after school tomorrow, before the demo?'

'Nothing. Why?'

Charlie smiled as she said it. 'We've got an idea.'

In the general room everybody clustered round Danny who was spelling out the timing.

'Here's the plan. We meet at four-fifteen at the Civic Centre, right?'

All agreed. Speedy saw Fraser in the far corner.

'You coming with us, Frase?'

Fraser thought about it.

'I don't know. I am sort of half official now.'

Winston grinned.

'That's okay. The half that's unofficial can come.'

Fraser decided.

'Yeah, why not? If they close this place down I lose my job anyway.'

As he crossed to join them Danny continued.

'Winston's dad's fetching the placards in his van. And another thing, no torn jeans and tatty T-shirts, we don't want them saying we're just a load of scruffy kids.'

Chrissie went for a wind-up.

'I could wear my Lycra jogging gear.'

And caught Danny nicely.

'You won't!'

Chrissie said it to Tessa.

'He doesn't like my jogging gear. He thinks it's provocative.'

The reply came from Tessa in a flash.

'Well, it is!' And everybody laughed.

The laughter died as PJ, arriving with Debbie in tow, crossed to Danny. He looked serious.

'Outside. Now.'

'Later, man. We're just going to have a last run through of the song.'

PJ was having no nonsense.

'Now.' He pointed at Winston, 'And you, Win,' followed by Fraser. 'Fraser too.'

Speedy called from where he stood at the back of the piano.

'What about me?'

'Especially you.'

Then Tessa and Chrissie said it together.

'What about us?'

PJ shook his head.

'Sorry. Men's talk.'

And ignoring their look of indignation, PJ was leading the rest of the gang outside.

Debbie stayed behind, and Nicola asked her the question.

'What's that all about?'

But Debbie decided not to say.


They found Lee kicking a football around in the grounds, and they had quickly surrounded him almost before he'd noticed.

Seeing them, Lee stopped the ball.

'What's up?'

Having been told on the way what was going on by PJ, all the boys were equally angry.

Danny went first. 'You are, mate. Up the creek without a paddle.'

And was closely followed by Winston.

'You revolting little scumbag . . .'

PJ picked it up. 'Of all the filthy, stinking tricks . . .'

Speedy was amazed.

'I could have broke me neck . . .'

Lee knew they had him but he decided to bluff it out.

'I don't know what you're on about.'

Fraser stepped right up to him before speaking.

'Nobbling Speedy's bike, that's what we're on about.'

Lee said, 'She's lying,' and, too late, realised his mistake as Danny picked it up.

'Who's lying?'

Lee's eyes darted from face to face looking for sympathy, there was none.

'Well. Must have been one of the girls, stands to reason. You know what little tell-tale cats they are.'

Winston spoke ominously.

'We know what you did.'

And PJ was equally contained.

'And we know about the threats to Debbie.'

Fraser quietly spelt it out.

'We know the whole story. I'm sure Geoff'd be very interested. Not to mention Debbie's dad.'

Lee tried to give a little laugh, it didn't work.

'It was only a joke. I wasn't to know she'd take it serious.'

Speedy wasn't having him wriggle out of it.

'It wasn't a joke about making me lose the race though, was it?'

Winston's comment was just as heartfelt.

'Yeah. And all our money.'

'Exactly how much did you win, sunshine?' PJ wanted to know.

Lee lied glibly. 'I don't remember.'

But Fraser knew the answer already.

'I know. Spuggie told me. Over sixty quid.'

PJ knew what was needed in reparation. 'Right. Hand it over.'

Again Lee lied.

'Haven't got it on me.'

Fraser wasn't having it.

'You heard the man. Hand it over.'

And they all moved in to surround him in a tight and threatening bunch.

Lee dipped his hand in his inside pocket as he spoke.

'This is blackmail, this is.'

PJ put his hand out and took the bundle, quickly counting it.

'Only thirty-five quid here.'

Lee's voice carried a plea for belief.

'I spent the rest. Honest.'

Not believing him they moved even closer.

And finally he brought the rest from his back trouser pocket.

Fraser took all the money and bundling it together passed it to Speedy.

'Right. Here you are, Speedy, mate. Towards your new bike.'

Speedy took it, quietly thrilled, as PJ spelt it out to Lee.

'We don't want to see you anywhere near here again, got that?'

Winston emphasised the threat.

'Or we fetch the law in.'

'One other thing,' Fraser added. 'Keep away from Debbie Dobson.'

With that the group moved back so Lee could walk from the circle. He tried to sneer but he couldn't quite bring it off.


The following day, after school was out, Spuggie set off for Charlie's house, full of a strange mix of excitement and tension. What was the invitation from Nicola and Charlie all about?

She soon found out. They were going to give her the most amazing make-up job that she had ever had in her life.

Arriving there, she found Nicola and Charlie waiting, and all three went straight to Charlie's bedroom. They sat her down on a chair facing the dressing-table mirror, put a make-up cape around her neck, and telling her to close her eyes, they began – Charlie applying the make-up and Nicola styling her hair.

While they worked on her, they took turns each at trying to guess who the lucky boy was who Spuggie fancied.

Charlie took first guess.

'I bet it's Duncan.'

Nicola thought she had it wrong.

'No, it's not, it's PJ.'

Charlie laughed.

'Can't be Winston.'

Then Nicola had another thought.

'Could be Danny.'

But Spuggie was dead set on keeping her secret.

'I've told you, I'm not doing it for a boy. I'm not interested in no stupid boys.'

Charlie placated her.

'All right, all right, whatever you say. Are you done, Nicola?'

'Two ticks. There.'

And Charlie, taking off the make-up cape, said the words that Spuggie had been waiting for.

'You can open your eyes now.'

Spuggie did. And she saw herself, transformed. Her eyes kept opening with the surprise of it. Inside her head Spuggie searched for the words to describe how she looked, and finally she found them.

'Really "nice".'

But Charlie wasn't quite finished.

'Hang on.'

And she dipped into her jewellery box and fished out a pair of pretty earrings, which she clipped onto Spuggie's ears.

'There. What do you think?'

Spuggie didn't know what to say. She had had no idea she could look like this. Finally she turned from the mirror to look from Nicola to Charlie before asking the question tentatively.

'Do you think Marcus'll like it?'

They both nodded their heads, quietly thrilled that Spuggie was so obviously pleased.

They would have been slightly less thrilled if they'd seen old Mr Doyle at that moment standing on his doorstep looking up and down the street to see if they were coming.

They hadn't got round to mentioning they were going to be late because of the demo.

Outside the Civic Centre the Grovers started to gather ready for the big moment. Winston was there handing out the placards from the back of his dad's van.

Chrissie, seeing Tessa approaching weighed down with a heavy holdall, called to her.

'Where've you been?'

'Library, I had to get some books for my project.'

Chrissie said it as Tessa reached her.

'What did you do, go in and ask if they've got any smelly old church books?'

When Tessa had met Chrissie outside the library the day before, she'd explained she was doing a project on old churches, much to Chrissie's amusement. Now it was Tessa's turn to smile.

'Smelly old buildings books, actually. I thought it'd widen the scope.'

Angel, having got two placards off of Winston, looked for someone to give one to, saw Noddy standing alone, watching. She went to join him.

'What you doing here?'

Noddy hunched his shoulders.

'Just watching.'

But Angel wasn't having that.

'Never mind just watching, you can carry this.' With that she shoved the placard at him, and he happily took it.

Standing by the kerb she asked him the question fascinated, and the conversation followed like a bullet.

'So why do they call you Noddy then?'

'Why do they call you Angel?'

'It's my name.'

'So. Mine's Noddy.'

'You were christened it. I baptise thee Noddy . . .'

'I have got another name but I'm not telling you.'

Angel was perplexed.

'Why not?'

Noddy shook his head.

'Don't want to.'

Angel egged him on.

'Go on. What is it? I won't tell. Cross my heart.'

There was a pause before Noddy finally said it:

'Norman.'

Angel was amazed.

'What?'

'Norman.'

And then he watched as she collapsed into a paroxysm of laughter that seemed would never end.

All Noddy could say glumly was, 'It's not that funny.'

Speedy was at the van but Winston wasn't passing him a placard, so he finally made the protest.

'Where's mine?'

Winston looked at Speedy's bandaged ankle.

'You can't march with your gammy leg.'

But Speedy was adamant.

'I've been going to Byker Grove ever since I came here. It's like me family. They're shutting it over my dead body.'

Winston saw it was a waste of time arguing.

'Right.'

And Winston felt it was an opportune moment to get something else off his mind.

'Speedy, man, I'm sorry for losing me rag when you fell off your bike. Blaming you for not getting it seen to at the shop.'

Speedy answered while trying to work out how to hold placard and crutch.

'That's all right. Probably should have done.'

But Winston wasn't having that.

'No. It was all his fault. Rotten little toad.'

'I don't suppose he knew I was going to come such a cropper.'

'You could have been killed, man.'

Speedy had had enough.

'Well, I wasn't, so shut it, right? Else you'll have me blubbing.'

A short distance away Danny had bumped into Chrissie, who was raring to go; and wanted the march to get underway. Danny said it without thinking.

'I don't know why you're so worked up about it. You've hardly been going to the Grove five minutes.'

Chrissie looked at him coolly.

'I hate anything that's unfair.'

Danny had to smile at the thought.

'Get away. You just like a good scrap.'

'I won't be trodden on by anybody, if that's what you mean.'

And Danny realised she meant it.

Fraser saw Spuggie arriving with Charlie and Nicola and couldn't contain his surprise at Spuggie's appearance.

'What the heck have you done to yourself?'

Spuggie was pleased he'd at least noticed there was something different.

'Charlie and Nicola did it,' and added tentatively, 'Do you like it?'

Fraser thought about it.

'Yes. Yes, I do. You look...'

'What?'

Fraser shook his head in amazement.

'Almost like a girl.'


PJ, having got a placard for himself and Debbie, took the opportunity of comforting her.

'You all right now?'

She nodded.

'He won't bother you again, I can promise you that.'

Debbie shook her head to indicate he'd got it wrong. 'It's not me I'm worried about. It's our Jemma. She might be a right little pain but she is my kid sister.'


And if Debbie had heard the conversation that Jemma was having with a sulking Lee at the top of the street she might have been even more worried.

'Hiya. You coming with us?'

'Where?' Lee said.

Jemma pointed down the street to the Town Hall.

'There.'

Lee sneered.

'Not likely.'

'Why not? You don't want 'em to close the Grove, do you?'

'I don't care if they burn it down.'

Jemma knew that all the Grovers were being totally unfair. If they knew the truth about his background they would have been much more understanding.

'I know they've got it in for you, but you want to take no notice. Our Debbie keeps trying to tell me these stupid stories but I just do this.'

Jemma covered her ears to demonstrate what she did when Debbie talked to her about him. Then she grabbed Lee's arm.

'Come on.'

'Where to?'

Jemma pointed down the street to where the march was just getting going.

'There.'

Outside the Civic Centre the Grovers were being marshalled into a ragged line by Winston and PJ.

Marcus caught sight of Angel's ADOMINABULL placard.

'You don't spell abominable like that.'

Angel smiled. 'I know. It's to make people notice. It worked with you, didn't it?'

Just then Spuggie passing by caught sight of Marcus who earlier had said he couldn't come, and her face beamed.

'Marcus! You came!'

'Somebody had to keep an eye on you. Don't want you clobbering the Mayor over the bonce with that thing.'

Spuggie laughed, then asked the question carefully.

'What do you think then?'

'What of?'

Disappointed Spuggie shrugged it off.

'Never mind.'

And Marcus puzzled over what it could be.


PJ shouted loud enough for all to hear.

'Right, we all fit? Okay, troops. Forward, march! Take it away, Charlie, girl!'

And as Charlie started singing their campaign song, soon everybody was joining in at the top of their voices.

At the tail end Jemma was trying to tug a reluctant Lee to join. He protested loudly.

'Get off. I don't want to.'

'Well, I want you to... We are friends, aren't we?'

When the marching reached the Town Hall they stopped marching, but carried on singing and hoisting their placards in the air, for the benefit of the camera crew who had turned up from BBC Television North.


Ian McDowell and Mr Bewick came out onto the step. Bewick's eyes scanned the gathered group angrily, then his eyes landed

103

on Marcus and stopped. Spuggie saw, and looking at Marcus saw that he was staring straight back at his father defiantly.

Ian saw that Geoff was there keeping a beady on the proceedings. He crossed to him.

'I'm surprised you're here, Geoff, as a public employee.'

Geoff was ready with his answer.

'Just as an observer, Ian. Does that give the council a problem?'

Ian shook his head.

'Not particularly. I was just mentioning it as a friend.' Then he got to the point.

'Would you pop in? We've got some news.'

Geoff nodded, then followed him to the door, and went in behind Mr Bewick who had obviously seen enough.

As the gang saw Geoff go through the front doors, the singing tailed off, and placards were lowered as a hush fell. It was Speedy, whose ankle was really aching, who called out:

'What do we do now?'

And PJ, of course, had the answer.

'Back to the Grove and wait with everything crossed. Come on, Debbie. Debs?' Getting no reply, he turned to look at her, she was staring horrified to the back of the group. PJ looked in that direction, and saw why she stared.

Jemma stood there, holding Lee's hand, and both of them stared back defiantly at Debbie.

There was an air of hushed expectancy in the general room as they all arrived back, and then sat around waiting for Geoff's return. Spuggie sitting in the corner with Marcus finally asked him the question.

'What'll happen with your dad?'

Marcus shrugged.

'Find out when I go home, won't I?'

Alison came in and saw them all.

'They didn't cart any of you off to jail, then?'

Winston laughed.

'You're joking, they were all on our side!'

At that point Jemma entered, and PJ remembered.

'Not all of 'em, Win.'

Debbie called to her.

'Jemma . . .'

But Jemma turned on her straight away.

'Just shut up. I know what you're going to say and it's none of your business.'

The whole room was suddenly involved in the discussion and the atmosphere was electric.

PJ didn't mince words.

'Debbie's right, you dope. You've got stop seeing that slimeball.'

Jemma turned her ire on PJ.

'You can't tell us what to do. Nobody can. Lee's my friend.'

Winston added his thoughts. 'He's poison, girl.' Then called across the room to Speedy who sat near the piano.

'Speedy, tell her what he did to you, man . . .'

Jemma clapped her hands over her ears.

'I won't listen . . .'

Fraser, having entered the room last, had heard it all, and now said it quietly.

'Be sensible, Jemma. That lad's best kept away from . . .'

Jemma was by now near to tears but adamant in her belief in him. She knew the truth, but Lee had sworn her to secrecy so she couldn't tell them his family's tragic secret, even though she was dying to, just to see their shame. But because she was a good and honest friend she couldn't let him down.

'It's not fair, you're all ganging up on him, but you don't know him like I do, none of you.'

She looked from face to face, searching for support, but didn't find it.

'Our Nicola's always going on about standing up for what you believe in. Well, I believe in Lee. So there.'

And with that she turned and ran out of the room. Alison, who had caught the tail end of it as she came from the office with a totally bald young man, asked Debbie:

'What was all that about?'

But Debbie just shook her head.

'Just one of Jemma's tantrums. I'll talk to her later.'

It was Spuggie who called the question at Alison, indicating the man.

'Who's that?'

Alison explained.

'Lloyd's starting a new course, if anyone's interested.' Then turned to Lloyd. 'Why don't you introduce yourself?'

Lloyd gave a smile that swept the room before he spoke.

'Thank you. Name's Lloyd, and I'm here to teach you a thing or two.'

Chrissie breathed in and did her deep, husky voice.

'You can teach me anything you want, any time!'

Lloyd wisely ignored the remark and the laughter that followed it.

'What I'm going to teach you will help you to function better, have more confidence, more coordination, be generally healthier and more relaxed. Though you lot look like if you were any more relaxed you'd be asleep.'

PJ leapt to their defence.

'We've been marching, man.'

And Winston backed him up.

'Yeah, we've got this big fight on our hands.'

Lloyd beamed again.

'Well then, looks like I'm just the guy you need.'


By the time Charlie and Nicola made Doyle's house, it had gone five o'clock.

He didn't take the chain off the hook as he opened the door in answer to their ring on the doorbell.

'What time d'you call this?'

Nicola started to apologise.

'We couldn't come earlier, we had to go to the Town Hall.'

And Charlie finished it.

'They're trying to close down our youth club, we all went to protest about it. And we didn't realise you were waiting.'

Doyle shook his head bad-temperedly.

'I wasn't! Better things to do with my time than sit here waiting for you.'

And before she could stop herself Charlie retorted tartly:

'Well, if you feel like that there's not much point in us coming any more, is there?'

He answered angrily, 'No, there isn't,' then started closing the door.

Nicola shouted: 'But, Doyle . . .'

But Doyle wasn't having any more of it.

'Go on, clear off. I don't need you. We're all right on us own, me and Nelson. Don't need nobody. Clear off.'

And with that he slammed the door closed.

As they walked up the path Nicola expressed her sorrow.

'Oh, heck, Charlie. We made a right mess of that.'

But Charlie wasn't having it.

'It's not your fault, Nic. He's impossible. At least you tried.'

If they had looked back, they would have seen Doyle sadly peering from behind the corner of his curtain, wishing he could call them back, but knowing his pride wouldn't let him.

At the Grove all the gang sat and hung on to Lloyd's every word.

'First, I want to be clear about this. Self-defence and Tai Chi are two separate things. Putting it simply, one is for health and relaxation, the other is what you might have to do to save your life. All right?'

It was Chrissie who got the question in first.

'Which are you going to teach us?'

Lloyd looked at her. 'Both. The biggest part of self-defence is using skill, balance and internal power and having confidence. Tai Chi improves health, vitality and coordination. So they go together.'

A thought struck Angel.

'Do you have to be big to do it?'

Lloyd shook his head.

'Not a bit. What do they call you, pet?'

'Angel.'

'Right, Angel. Tai Chi's not about physical strength, so it's ideally suited for titches like you . . .'

At which point Nicola walked in talking loudly to Charlie.

'Well, that's definitely it. I've done with Doyle for good.'

Charlie didn't believe her.

'You said that before.'

Nicola was adamant.

'I mean it this time. He can stew.'

At which everybody hushed them both loudly. Nicola realised they had burst in on something.

'What's going on?'

Danny called from the piano where he sat.

'Tai Chi. Sit down and listen.'

As Charlie and Nicola found seats Lloyd continued.

'You don't need lots of big strong muscles and height, what you do is you use your opponent's strength against them.'


Jemma had gone searching for Lee and finally found him in a grove of trees. They had sat together and chatted for a while. Jemma's next question, 'Tell me about them,' made Lee stop and think. 'Who?'

'Your little brothers and sisters. What are they called?'

Lee smiled and told her.

'Jack and Jill. They're the twins.'

'Twins!'

Lee nodded, pleased.

'Yeah. And Tom, he's the baby.'

He laughed at the thought.

'We call him Tom Thumb.'

Jemma smiled at his joy.

'I bet he's real sweet.'

Lee was surprised.

'I thought you didn't like babies?'

'I like other people's. I just don't like our own.'

Lee shook his head bemused.

'You've not got it yet.'

Jemma said it, heartfelt.

'I know what'll happen when it comes, though.'

'What?'

She looked at him before saying it.

'They'll all fuss over it and say "ah, isn't it cute" and they'll buy it things and spoil it and...'

And as the truth of the matter struck her she felt tears at the back of her eyes.

'... they won't have any time for me.'

In the general room Lloyd had wasted no time. As soon as he saw they were all interested in having a go, he got them doing simple Tai Chi exercises. Geoff walked in just as the exercises got underway. As soon as Alison saw the look on his face she couldn't stop herself but say it.

'Geoff?'

Slowly as the Grovers saw him standing there they stopped their exercising till Lloyd was left doing it by himself. Alison saying, 'I'm sorry, Lloyd...' stopped him. He looked to Geoff and realising there was a problem said it quietly.

'That's okay.'

Alison crossed over to Geoff.

'What happened?'

No reply. Geoff simply looked from face to face.

PJ couldn't bear the silence.

'Well, Geoff, man, what gives?'

Danny chipped in hopefully, 'Did we win?'

The silence held as Geoff gathered the words together. When he finally spoke his voice carried a weariness and a depth of sadness that they had never before experienced coming from Geoff, who they all looked to as a permanent pillar of strength.

When he spoke, carefully and slowly, it was the voice of defeat they were hearing.

'It was a good effort, kids. You did well. But it's not always true that faith can move mountains. Prestige Properties have made the council an offer they can't refuse. Subject to the legal formalities and a surveyor's report, they'll want to start work as soon as possible.'

A shocked silence hung like a pall over the room, then Winston finally asked it for all of them.

'What does that mean for us?'

Geoff shook his head, as if to deny the words he was about to say, but there was no denying them.

'It means, Winston, that within a very few weeks, we'll all be out of here... For good.'

# CHAPTER FIVE

In the days following the announcement a sort of doom-ridden gloom settled over the Grovers. Geoff didn't let them know he was checking out a variety of alternative meeting places that Ian was putting on offer, for the very good reason that what he was seeing was so unsuitable and depressing compared with the Grove, that he didn't want to make the gang even more miserable by showing them the sort of place they could expect to end up in.

A week after Geoff's announcement Spuggie's spirits were lifted momentarily when she received a letter from her friend Joanne in America with an amazing offer. Then, realising there was no way she could possibly afford to accept the offer, she tried putting it out of her mind, but it wasn't an easy thing to forget. Bumping into Marcus on her way home from school that night she got the grumble off her chest straight away.

'Have you fell out with us or what?'

She noticed that Marcus was a bit shifty when he replied.

'Of course not.'

'Then why have you not been to the Grove?'

'Why do you think?'

'Your dad?'

'He wasn't pleased.'

'You shouldn't let him boss you.'

Marcus flushed at her comment. She had no idea what it was really like at home.

'I don't need you telling me what to do, thank you.'

'Suit yourself.'

She was about to walk away when she changed her mind and decided to share the thought that had been buzzing round her head all day.

'I've had a letter from Joanne. She's my friend in America. Used to live with us till her real dad turned up.'

'What does she say?'

'She wants me to go and stay with them. She says we can go to Disneyland.'

'Hey, that's great!'

'No, it's not. I can't afford to go to Whitley Bay, never mind Disneyland.'

Marcus gave her his nicest smile.

'Still. Nice to be asked, eh?'

Spuggie smiled in return, and knew they were back to being friends again.

Getting back from his latest forage through the world of empty council properly, Geoff broke the news to Alison and Fraser that yet again the place had been a dump.

'It's adequate. It'd do. But it's not Byker Grove.'

Fraser tried looking on the bright side.

'It'd be better than nothing.'

And Alison's remark was even more to the point.

'We're going to have to be positive about it, Geoff. Prestige Properties were on the phone earlier. They're bringing a surveyor round this afternoon.'

Geoff's reply came glumly.

'Not wasting any time, are they?'

Debbie had other worries on her mind apart from the imminent loss of the Grove. She finally shared them with Nicola.

'She's still seeing him.'

She had spotted Jemma the night before coming out of the early pictures with Lee, they hadn't seen her, but she hadn't missed the fact that they now walked hand in hand everywhere. Nicola stated the obvious.

'You know our pig-headed little Jemma. The more we tell her not to do it the more she will.'

'Do you think we should tell Mam?'

Nicola had no hesitation.

'No. She's got enough to worry about right now. She's being sick every morning.'

Debbie shook her head in disbelief.

'You think God would have found a better way of organising babies, wouldn't you? Poor old Mam.'

Nicola said, jokingly:

'You mean go into the supermarket and buy one over the counter?' Debbie giggled.

'Brilliant! Then if it turned out to be a right little pest like our Jemma you could take it back and change it.'

Their laughter was cut short by the arrival of their gran; in tears.

Nicola said it for both of them.

'What is it, Gran?'

Mary dried her eyes as she spoke, directing her remark at Nicola.

'I'm afraid I've got some bad news for you, pet.'

And what she had to say made Nicola leave the house, and dash to find Charlie.

Jemma was standing by the library gates looking up and down the road impatiently, when Tessa came out of the library loaded down with books and stopped to chat.

'Hiya. If you're coming to the Grove you can help me with this lot – they weigh a ton.' Jemma, not pleased to see her, looked at the bag she was carrying before asking.

'What are they?'

'Gold bars. I've just robbed a bank.'

In the face of Jemma's withering look she told her.

'Books. I've got this project to finish. Now will you help or do you want the titles first?'

Jemma shook her head.

'Sorry. I can't.'

Tessa set off as she made the remark sarcastically, 'Thanks. I'll do you a favour some time.'

At that moment Jemma saw Lee approaching, and she called to him.

'I've been waiting ages.'

He called back.

'Been shopping.'

When he arrived at her side he thrust a small package into her hand, a bit embarrassed.

'Here.'

'What is it?'

'Open it.'

She did so and was amazed. It was a beautiful, sparkly bracelet. Her eyes shone as she said:

'For me?'

Lee grinned.

'Well, it's certainly not for me.'

She just couldn't believe it.

'It's not my birthday.'

Lee shrugged.

'Doesn't have to be a reason, does there?'

But Jemma knew better.

'Yes, there does.'

And she looked at him, until Lee finally told her.

'It's for sticking by us when they were all having a go.'

And as Jemma put the bracelet on, she realised all the Grovers didn't know just how unfair they were being to him. Nobody else had ever bought her a present when it wasn't her birthday.


At the Grove, Charlie, Kelly, Angel and Chrissie were sorting through an old dressing-up box, full of tatty clothes, as PJ and Winston played darts off in the corner.

Chrissie took a bedraggled dress out and held it against her.

'And here's Christina modelling a moth-eaten little number from the trendy bag-lady range.'

Charlie smiled, recognising it.

'Speedy wore that in the Christmas panto.'

Chrissie grinned.

'Bet it was just his colour.'

At that moment Spuggie and Marcus walked in, Marcus carrying his telescope. Spuggie wondered out loud what the girls were up to, and Kelly told her.

'Geoff wants us to start sorting stuff out ready for the move.'

Angel plonked a hat on Spuggie's head, and smiled as she said it.

'Suits you, that.'

Spuggie threw it back in the box.

'Get off! I bet it's full of fleas.'

She saw Fraser heading for the tea bar.

'Fraser! Geoff says you've got to come with us. We're going to put Marcus's telescope on the roof, and he's afraid one of us might fall off.'

Fraser grinned as he said it.

'One of you might get *pushed* off; and I know which one it's likely to be.'

Hearing what was going on, Kelly dropped the dress she was holding back in the box and stood.

'Can I come?'

Angel was back on her feet as well.

'Me too!'

Fraser got his remark in quick before a stampede developed.

'Okay. But that's enough. I can't have hundreds of you swarming about up there.'

As they all headed for the stairs, Nicola came in red-eyed and upset and scanned the room looking for Charlie. Catching sight of her by the clothes box, she crossed to her side but at first couldn't speak. Seeing her standing there looking like that, Charlie knew something was very wrong.

'What is it, Nic?'

It was moments before Nicola could manage to say it, but finally she did.

'Doyle's dead.'

Charlie was shocked beyond belief.

'What!'

Nicola's tears were flowing as she spoke.

'He fell and broke his hip, Charlie. He lay there for hours and nobody knew. The home-help found him.'

'Oh, Nic. That's awful.'

'If only we'd not stopped going to see him. We could have got him to hospital.'

Charlie refused to accept the argument.

'We didn't know that.'

And then another thought struck her.

'Remember he said he was going to die? He obviously had a ... what's that word?'

Chrissie, who had been listening, fascinated, threw it in.

'Presentiment?'

Charlie nodded.

'Yes. That's the one.'

But Nicola wasn't having it.

'I don't believe in that stuff. It was just the way he was.'

She sobbed as she said it.

'Rotten old misery.'

Charlie took her hand comfortingly as she spoke.

'It wasn't our fault, Nic.'

But Nicola wasn't to be comforted.

'We should have been there to help. But we weren't and he died in pain, alone. Poor old unhappy Doyle.'

And with that she sobbed on Charlie's shoulder.


On the way upstairs with the telescope group, Kelly saw Tessa who was pouring over her books in the peace of one of the upper rooms. Tessa rather than accepting Kelly's invitation to go with them, strangely excited, asked Kelly to come into the room and close the door. She did and crossed to the table where Tessa sat.

There was no disguising her excitement as she spoke.

'Listen to this.'

Kelly saw she was looking at a book.

'What is it?'

'It's about old buildings. It's got this place in it. Seems parts of it go back hundreds of years. Some priors had a chapel here in 1453; then it was sold as a private house.'

'Yuck! I wouldn't want to live here. I mean it's all right for a club ...'

But Tessa didn't give her time to finish the thought.

'The point is there's a priest hole somewhere. Probably under the foundations.' Now Tessa was really getting worked up.

'Kelly. Anything could be down there.'

Kelly pulled a face.

'Yeah. Spiders, rats. Bats ...'

But Tessa had a more positive list.

'. . . Crucifixes, goblets, jewels even.'

Kelly shook her head and shivered as she said it.

'Piles of mouldy old bones more like.'

But Tessa wasn't going to be sidetracked.

'It's history, Kelly. It'd really make my project to find something like that.'

Kelly suddenly saw where the conversation was leading.

'You're never thinking of looking for it!?'

'Why not?'

'Geoff would go bonkers for one.'

'Who says Geoff has to know?'

And it finally dawned on Kelly that that was exactly what Tessa was going to do:

Go hunting the hidden priest hole in the sub-basement of Byker.

On the roof Marcus soon had the telescope set up, and while he was checking the focus Angel pulled at his coat.

'What can you see? Let us have a look, go on.'

Spuggie was adamant.

'Me first. It was my idea.'

Fraser stated the obvious.

'I don't know what you're both squabbling over; you won't be able to see a thing till it's dark anyway.'

Marcus gave a groan and said, 'Oh no!'

Swinging the telescope round he'd caught sight of something at the gate he could well do without.

It was Spuggie who asked the question.

'What is it?'

'My dad's car. Him and a couple of chaps in it.'

Angel was perplexed.

'I thought you were supposed to be looking at the sky?'

Ignoring her, Spuggie picked Marcus's comment up.

'Is he coming here?'

He nodded his head.

'Worse luck.'

But Spuggie was on her way, calling as she went.

'Come on! Let's go and see what they want!'

And Angel went dashing off after her.

Fraser said:

'I'll have to be getting back too.'

But Marcus didn't make a move.

'You go then. I'm stopping.'

'Marcus. I can't leave you up here on your own. We'll come back when it's dark.' But Marcus's face was set.

'I'm not going down, Fraser, not while he's here.'

Fraser thought about it.

'I had a dad I could do without seeing a lot of the time.'

'Spuggie told me. She said he used to beat up on you.'

'When he could catch me.'

Marcus shook his head.

'Mine's never hit me. It's his tongue. He has this way of making you feel dead useless. You know? Nothing you do is ever good enough.'

Fraser had a lot of sympathy for him, and even though it was breaking the rules he finally gave way.

'Okay. But don't go too near the edge or I'm out of a job.'

'I won't.'

Fraser headed for the door, but Marcus's call stopped him. 'Fraser?'

Fraser turned to look at him.

'Thanks.'

As Fraser went, Marcus looked down and saw his father and colleagues getting out of the long black car, and he wondered whether, if he had had a plant pot, he would have dropped it on him.


By a bit of bad timing, Amanda had arrived at the Grove just before her dad, and everyone was making a great point of ignoring her arrival. Alison crossed to chat to her.

'Hello, Amanda. Glad you came back.'

Amanda looked round the room glumly.

'Nobody else is.'

'They'll get over it.'

At that moment Spuggie and Angel flew down the stairs, Spuggie shouting it as she came.

'Mr Bewick and those men are back!'

Angel chipping in, 'Seen them from the roof!'

Before anyone could say anything Geoff was leading the three men into the room. Seeing her dad Amanda wished she could die on the spot. Alison saw the look on her face.

'You're not responsible for your dad's job, pet.'

The men faced the gathered children, and the animosity was palpable. It was Winston who said it to Geoff, speaking for all of them.

'What do they want?'

But it was Mr Bewick who answered him, trying to be friendly but instead coming over oily.

'Well, son. These two gentlemen are going to do a detailed survey. Don't worry, we won't get in your way.'

At that moment he caught sight of Amanda and called to her brightly.

'Hello, Princess.'

And once more she wished the floor would open and swallow her up. It didn't, so she answered, 'Hello,' hoping that was the end of it. It wasn't. He smiled.

'I trust you did your homework before you came out, young lady?'

'Yes, sir.'

He turned to the two men, beaming.

'Brains and beauty, not bad, eh?'

And Amanda realised that every eye in the Grove was watching her.

It was Winston who had the brilliant idea.

'Er, Geoff?'

'Yes?'

Winston said it innocently enough.

'I hope you remember to tell the gentlemen about the rot in the window frames?' Then he aimed it directly at Mr Bewick.

'We've been trying to get the council to fix it, but they say it's too big a job.'

PJ caught on and added his comment.

'Whole lot's gone right through the building. Dry rot or something they call it.' Bewick looked at them both, not sure if he was being wound up or not.

'Thanks for mentioning it, son.'

As he crossed to leave the room with the men, the whole gang made their mind up as one, and set off to follow them. Debbie in passing said to Amanda sarcastically, 'Ta-ta, Princess.'

And Amanda fought her tears.

In the kitchen Mary was buttering bread when the invasion arrived. Geoff introduced her to the three men, then Winston was at it again.

'The poor lady's always complaining about the damp in here, aren't you, Mrs O'Malley?'

Mary looked at him blankly.

'Am I?'

PJ tried to get the message across.

'You say it gets your arthritis twinges going.'

And she finally cottoned on.

'Oh the damp! Yes, something shocking.'

By which time, having seen enough, the men were ready to leave the room and head upstairs, and the gang were all set to follow, but Geoff barred their way with his arm across the door.

'Nice try. But don't push it, eh?'

Then he followed the men upwards.

Marcus heard the voices floating up the stairs, and recognised his father's straight away, but there was no place to hide. Then his father was there, and saw Marcus. He spoke over-cheerily.

'Can't seem to go anywhere without tripping over my two sprogs today.'

Then he crossed to stand by Marcus and looked at the view.

'Good vantage point.'

Marcus simply nodded.

'Not as good as Mount Kenya, though, hey?'

Again Marcus didn't speak. His father gave him one final cool glance. Then spoke to the others.

'Right. We must bash on.'

As they went Geoff crossed to Marcus, there was an edge of anger in his voice.

'Fraser had no right to leave you up here on your own.'

'Don't blame him. I asked him to.'

And then the worrying thought struck Marcus.

'He won't get into trouble, will he?'

Geoff shook his head.

'Not this time.'

Marcus was relieved.

'I didn't want to come down.'

Geoff totally understood.

'I know. But I think you best had now. With me.'

Marcus nodded, and he and Geoff crossed to the stairs together.

In the interim the Grovers had gone back to their previous occupation in the general room, but it was almost eerily quiet. Debbie and Kelly folded old clothes from the dressing-up box, while PJ and Charlie sorted through tapes. Angel and Noddy took posters off the wall, and Speedy and Winston came in from the games room carrying old equipment which they added to the pile growing in the centre of the room, that was due for chucking out. Alison and Fraser watched sadly from the snack bar.

The only noise came from Danny who sat at the piano gently touching a series of chords that spelt out his sorrow.

Amanda viewed the silent activity, and then bravely crossed to Debbie.

'Can I help?'

Debbie was all ready to say 'No,' when she saw Alison had her eye on her. Begrudgingly she agreed.

'If you want.'

And pleased to have something to do, Amanda knelt and started folding clothes with them.

This was the scene that met Mr Bewick on his return with the two men. All eyes turned on them as they entered and the silence was almost menacing. Mr Bewick spoke loudly trying to break through the wall of animosity.

'Soon be out of your hair now, kids.'

Geoff and Marcus also arrived, and they sensed the tension in the room which was almost electric.

It was Winston who started it. He rocked back on his heels and they made a drumming noise on the floor, and he continued to do so rhythmically. Soon, one by one, the others joined in and the noise started to swell in volume.

Only Marcus and Amanda were not doing it. Then without a word being spoken, and still keeping up the rhythm with their heels, the Grovers started to link arms making a solid chain that ran across the room.

Bewick turned on Geoff angrily, shouting to be heard above the racket.

'Aren't you going to stop this nonsense?!'

Geoff said it quietly.

'They're not breaking any rules.'

Mr Bewick was about to leave, when Marcus made his way past him, and then, without taking his eyes off his father, went to link arms with Spuggie at one end of the chain and soon his heels were making as much noise as anyone.

Mr Bewick was flushed with anger, he looked to Amanda. For a moment she hesitated, and then she too crossed to Debbie at the other end, Debbie took the arm she offered and let her join the chain.

When Bewick spoke it was loud and icy, and directed straight at Marcus.

'I shall see you at home.'

And with that he turned and leaving his two companions standing there, angrily slammed out of the building.

But as he walked to the car the noise of the banging continued to echo in his ears.

At the Dobsons', Mary sat in her usual chair and mused over

the events of the day that she'd watched from the tea bar window, for Jemma's benefit.

'All that anger and nothing nobody could do. I wanted to go up to those men and say, "Go away. Leave us alone. Let Byker Grove be!"'

Jemma thought it must have been a thrilling moment.

'I wish I'd been there.'

Debbie was just coming into the room as Jemma spoke.

'So where were you, anyroad?'

Jemma felt herself blush. Twice in a row she had been to the pictures with Lee, and neither time had they paid. The first time Lee had shown her how to use a bit of wire to get in the exit door at the back; the second time he'd got her to try it, and she'd succeeded. Lee had explained it wasn't really stealing. The picture was going on in any case, and they just helped to make the audience a bit larger.

'Well?'

Debbie's question cut through her thoughts, and she replied on automatic.

'None of your business.'

Debbie almost spat it at her.

'You were with that scumbag.'

Jemma was furious.

'Just shut it, you!'

She had jabbed a finger angrily at Debbie as she spoke, and Debbie caught sight of the bracelet at her wrist.

'Where'd you get that?'

And once more Jemma retreated to the old favourite.

'None of your business.'

Debbie sneered.

'Who'd he rob this time?'

But Jemma had had just about enough.

'I hate you! I do! You're horrible!'

Mary tried to break it up.

'Debbie, Jemma, don't start again. Your mam's having a lie down and you're not to upset her, you hear me?'

Any further argument was stopped in its tracks by the arrival of Nicola. Or rather stopped in its tracks at amazement at what Nicola had brought with her.

She was carrying a cage, and inside the cage was a very mangy parrot. Nelson.

'What the heck's that?' Debbie said.

Jemma answered sarcastically.

'Looks like a parrot to me.'

But Debbie could handle that.

'I can see it's a parrot – but whose is it?'

Nicola said softly, 'Doyle's.'

And then immediately amended it.

'It was Doyle's.'

As they fussed over it, asking if it could speak and making parrot noises at it, Nicola remembered what she had done after leaving the Grove. She had gone to stand in front of Doyle's house; stood there, almost willing him to appear. And then, through her tears, hoping that somehow he could hear her, she had said it softly.

'I'm sorry, Doyle. I'm so sorry.'

Marcus and Amanda were in no great hurry to leave the Grove that evening, all that was waiting for them at home was trouble, but finally the moment arrived when they could put it off no longer. As they set off down the drive Marcus said,

'Thanks, Mand.'

She looked at him.

'What for?'

'You know – joining the chain.'

She smiled.

'I couldn't let you do it by yourself.'

Then the smile left her face.

'Are you scared?'

Marcus nodded.

'A bit.'

'Me too.'

Marcus said it without rancour.

'He won't do anything to you. He never does.'

He pictured the earlier confrontation in his mind's eye, his father's furious face, and realised he was pleased.

'I'm glad I let him know he can't always tell me what to think and what to do.'

And with that Marcus took Amanda's hand, and with a quickened pace they set off to face whatever there was to face.

Tessa and Kelly were also still in the grounds, sitting on the play frame in earnest conversation. When Tessa had told her she intended to go searching for the way to the priest hole underneath the cellar, Kelly had been adamant.

'I'd not let you go down there on your own.'

'I don't think I'd be too wild about that neither.'

Then Kelly had a thought.

'We could ask one of the boys. Say Speedy or Winston?'

Tessa shook her head.

'Might as well broadcast it on "News at Ten".'

'What about PJ then?'

Tessa considered it.

'Yeah. Maybe PJ can keep a secret.'

And so it was decided. If he agreed they would get the project underway as soon as possible.

Next day, after school had finished, Spuggie lay in wait for Marcus once more.

He smiled when he saw her.

'Another letter from America?'

'Give us a chance! I've not wrote back to her last one yet.'

'What will you say?'

There was touch of sadness in her voice.

'That I can't go.'

She shook the mood off with a change of subject.

'What happened with your dad?'

'The usual. Sixty lashes, and bread and water for a month.'

Seeing the horrified look on Spuggie's face he smiled and put it right.

'I'm only joking, he's not that bad.'

'So what did he do?'

'Gave us a right old earbashing and stopped my pocket money.'

Spuggie was incensed.

'That's not fair!'

Marcus explained.

'He said I'd been insolent. He reckons I've not been showing respect. He's very hot on showing respect, is my dad. Should have been a sergeant major.'

'What about Amanda?'

Marcus had to smile in spite of himself as he remembered.

'She was just copying her big bad brother according to him. She tried telling him but he doesn't listen.'

Then the ongoing unfairness struck him and he fell silent.

After a while Spuggie went for a change of subject again.

'If you're coming back to the Grove, you could show me some more stars tonight. It's going to be clear.'

He looked at her and smiled.

'You a weather expert now?'

She smiled back.

'I read the forecast. You said we'd be able to see cassiewhatsit if there's no clouds.

'Cassiopeia.'

Then she saw she had sparked his interest.

'Might even get a look at Saturn if we're lucky.'

'Is that the one with all the rings?'

He looked at her with a new respect.

'You *have* been reading it up.'

Then his mind was made up.

'Okay. See you there then.'

Spuggie was thrilled.

'Promise?'

'Promise. Even if he locks us in the dungeon and throws away the key.'

And with that, Spuggie went happily on her way.

Byker Grove was slowly changing from its usual friendly chaos to a sort of 'ready to depart' orderliness, and those who continued to sort it out worked silently in teams of two and three.

Angel and Noddy took the last poster down, and the walls were then totally bare, with only the slightly cleaner paintwork behind showing there had ever been anything stuck there in the first place. Boxes piled high in the centre of the room were crammed with yesterday's memories, ready for transportation to any new venue that might finally turn up.

Chrissie came in and looked round the room. After watching Speedy and Winston, Danny, Debbie, Charlie and the rest working for a while, she finally spoke loudly, cutting through the gloom-laden silence.

'Good golly Miss Molly! Who died?'

They all looked in her direction, slightly shocked, as if she'd laughed out loud at a funeral or something.

As ever, whenever it was Chrissie who needed putting down, it was Danny who was first in the queue.

'That's all we need – a comedian.'

But Chrissie wasn't going to be put down.

'Oh do me a favour! So we have to move somewhere else? It's not the end of the world!'

Winston said it for all of them.

'It's different for you. You've not been coming here five minutes.'

But still Chrissie persisted in getting her message across.

'It's only a building, for heaven's sake! Surely the Grove's more than just bricks and stone? It's all the people who come here. They'll be the same wherever we go.'

The silence held as they all digested what she'd said. It was Danny who for once admitted begrudgingly, 'I suppose she's got a point.'

Chrissie pushed home her small advantage.

'Instead of moping around like a bunch of wet lettuces, why don't we organise something?'

Speedy thought about it.

'Like another march, you mean?'

'No, Speedy – I mean something to cheer us up.'

Winston had the answer.

'United are playing home Saturday, we could go mob-handed?'

Angel didn't fancy that.

'I hate football. Dead boring.'

Winston turned on her.

'And who asked you to come?'

But Noddy leapt to her defence gallantly.

'She can come if she wants.'

Chrissie took over again.

'I've got a better idea.'

And Danny, as if to make up for saying she could be right earlier, tried to score a point.

'Surprise, surprise.'

But Speedy, who had had just about enough of Danny's churlishness when it came to Chrissie, wasn't having that.

'Shut it, man! Let the girl speak.'

And he did, and then she did, and suddenly life looked as though it could be fun again.


At that moment in the empty games room, Tessa and Kelly watched, fascinated, as PJ fixed the window, so they could get in that evening after everyone had gone home.

Having swore him to secrecy, PJ had agreed to their plan quickly enough when they told him what it was. He wasn't sure there would be treasure trove involved if they did find the priest hole, but he didn't want to take a chance on missing out if by any chance there was.

He was now using Blu Tac, so the window latch didn't close properly, but looked as though it was. Tessa asked the obvious.

'What happens if Geoff sees it when he's doing his rounds?'

'He won't. It looks as though it's locked.' Having checked his handiwork he stepped back. 'Right, that's it. We meet up outside just after nine as soon as he's gone.'

Tessa was a bit miffed.

'I'm in charge of this!'

'Yeah. But I'm the one who knows where the trapdoor in the cellar is.'

Tessa saw he had a point.

PJ continued.

'And don't forget your torches.'

And then added a hopeful wind-up.

'And a bag to put the treasure in.'

Kelly went owl-eyed behind her glasses at the thought.

'You don't really think there'll be treasure?'

PJ, seeing he'd hooked her, went for it.

'We might find the odd skull.'

But they both looked so terrified at the thought, he decided to let them off the hook. He said it with a smile.

'Only joking. Let's go.'

They headed back to the general room, and discovered everyone excitedly talking about the skating party that had been suggested by Chrissie, much to Danny's disgust. He hadn't exactly excelled last time, and said he wouldn't be going. Spuggie also turned it down, coming over mysteriously as to what she was getting up to.

Winston blew it for her by calling out:

'Snogging with Lord Snooty on the roof, I shouldn't wonder!' Which really got Spuggie tearing into him.

While the commotion was going on Nicola meandered in with what was rapidly becoming her constant companion.

As Debbie saw her she called out:

'Do you have to cart that manky thing everywhere you go now?'

But everyone else was fascinated, and gathered round the cage as Nicola and Charlie told the story of Doyle.

Geoff saw the parrot as soon as he entered the room with Alison.

'Who's this then, a new member?'

Which, as it turned out, wasn't much short of the truth. Nicola explained.

'It's Doyle's parrot. There's no one to look after it.'

Jemma piped in.

'And we can't have it at home because of the stupid baby.'

Jemma saw from the instant glower from Nicola and Debbie that she had blown their secret.

Surprised at what Jemma had said, Alison asked the question.

'What baby?'

And one by one with machine gun rapidity, the Grovers told her.

Angel started it. 'Their baby.'

'Their mam's having another one,' Winston said.

'It's going to be born in April,' Speedy added.

'They're hoping for a little boy this time,' Spuggie went on.

And Angel finished it. 'If it is they're calling it Stephen.'

Jemma, Debbie and Nicola exchanged an amazed glance, then all three roared with laughter.

Spuggie was bemused.

'What's so funny?'

And it was Nicola who explained it.

'Well – it was supposed to be a secret between the three of us, Spug.'

Alison smiled at the thought.

'Well, you should know better. Congratulations anyway – that's wonderful news.'

Jemma put her straight.

'No, it's not! That's why me gran says we can't have the parrot pecking around the place.'

It took a lot of persuading on all their parts to get Geoff to agree to it being kept at the Grove.

'We'll all be homeless soon, never mind the parrot!'

But he finally relented.

'Okay then. I suppose it can stop while we've still got a roof over our heads.'

And there was general cheering all round.

At that moment Lloyd, the new instructor, arrived as agreed to give them their first proper Tai Chi lesson. But first he gave a blushing Alison a small bunch of flowers. Every eye was on them as she spoke.

'What are these for?'

And his suitably enigmatic reply, 'Because it's Thursday,' had everybody gathered, grinning.

Lloyd soon put a stop to that.

'Right, kids. Ready when you are.'

Up on the roof, Fraser watched Marcus focusing his telescope as the sun faded from view and evening slowly waned to night. It was a beautiful clear sky and Fraser knew it was going to be a wonderful experience for Spuggie to peer into the depths of the universe. As he thought his thoughts Marcus looked towards the door, and Fraser guessed at it.

'Spuggie'll be here in a minute. They're just finishing the Tai Chi.'

Marcus spoke as he finished focusing.

'It's a pity about America.'

Fraser agreed. But also knew his intentions for her. 'One of these days she'll get to go – when I make a lot of money.'

At which point Spuggie appeared in the doorway gasping and out of breath after taking the steps two at a time.

Her timing was perfect. As she arrived the sun slipped totally from view and the pre-moon sky was a soft blue velvet pool with only pinprick starlight specks to light the night.

Spuggie had hardly got her breath back before she said to Fraser:

'You don't have to stop, you know.'

But Fraser smiled and shook his head.

'Oh yes, I do, little sister – rules is rules.'

Marcus, at the telescope again, called:

'Spuggie! Look.'

She crossed to look, speaking as she did so.

'What am I looking for?'

'Cygnus the swan. It's a giant constellation spreading right across the northern Milky Way.'

A moment, then Spuggie gave an excited cry.

'I've got it! All those stars so close! You think you could reach out and touch them.'

Fraser and Marcus exchanged a glance, both pleased at Spuggie's excitement.

Realising that he could trust Fraser not to make fun of him, Marcus shared the memory.

'Once, just after I'd gone to Kenya, I saw a supernova. It was the brightest for a hundred years, like the hugest, brightest star you ever saw. It was magic.'

'You must have just have been a kid.'

'Ten. But I was hooked. On a clear dark night it's as if you leave the Earth and go up there. And one day I will.'

Spuggie had been listening, sharing the moment.

'How?'

'I want to get on the space programme.'

And they both realised he was being totally sincere.

Chrissie had been right that going skating would get everybody's mind off their misery. Everybody had a great time, and helped each other as best they could, the ones who could do it well, helping those who were beginners. Even Amanda was genuinely enjoying herself for the very first time, and when Debbie slipped and fell with a 'Whoops!' Amanda was there to offer her hand and Debbie took it without hesitation.

Jemma was also having a great time skating along hand in hand with Angel and Noddy, but seeing something she let go and shot off, and Angel and Noddy crashed into each other and fell to the ice with an accompanying yell.

Angel called after her.

'What did you do that for?!'

But Jemma had gone. She'd seen Lee at the barrier and raced in that direction, calling as she went.

'Hi! Lee! Over here!'

But when she arrived Lee was angry with her.

'You didn't tell me it was a set up!'

'What do you mean?'

He pointed to the gang.

'I didn't know that that lot was going to be here!'

'I want you all to be friends.'

'Look! They don't want to be mates with me any more than I want to be mates with them.'

As they stood at the barrier arguing, Debbie looked in that direction and saw them, and then called out angrily to Lee:

'Hey, you!'

Lee saw Debbie heading for them as quickly as she could manage, closely followed by Nicola who had also spotted him. Once more he turned on Jemma.

'See?'

And with that he turned and went, leaving Jemma screaming after him.

'Lee! Wait for us!'

But he just kept going. Jemma sat down on the step and started unlacing her boots.

Nicola, arriving at her side shortly before Debbie who she had overtaken, spoke softly.

'Debbie's right, Jem – let him go.'

But Jemma wasn't having it.

'You're a good one to talk. You wouldn't let nobody talk you out of going out with that Paul thingy; and he had the police after him.'

'And he caused me a lot of grief. I wish I had listened to them now.'

Jemma got her boots off and stood angrily.

'Go away! You don't know anything! So just leave us alone!'

And with that she was off, leaving Debbie and Nicola staring after her.

It was about this time that Kelly and Tessa arrived to join PJ under a bush in the Byker grounds waiting for the big moment when the lights would go off and Geoff would be on his way home. They had all dressed warmly and, as agreed, had a torch each with them. Now all they had to do was wait patiently.

At that moment Geoff was calling up the stairs to the roof level.

'Oy! You three star-gazers! Time we weren't here!'

Fraser called back from the distance:

'We're just coming!'

Now lit by the bright light of the recently risen crescent moon, Marcus had just about dismantled the telescope all ready to put it in its case.

'Won't be a tick, Fraser.'

Fraser nodded.

'I'll go on, but make sure you come straight down.'

Spuggie gave a 'Tch!' of disbelief that he could treat them like kids.

As Fraser went she crossed to the edge of the parapet, and stood looking up into the night sky. When he had finished packing the telescope away, Marcus joined her.

'What do you see?'

When she spoke it was with a sense of awe.

'The moon. The stars. All those things I know are there; because you've told me.'

It was a moment before he spoke.

'Fly up there in your mind's eye, Spuggie. Past the moon, beyond Mars and Jupiter, past Saturn and Uranus, past the comets and out beyond the nearest star; sail right across the solar system into all the other galaxies . . . isn't it breathtaking?'

She turned to look at him.

'It's wonderful.'

She didn't dare to say it, but said it anyway.

'And you're wonderful.'

And then, not knowing that Marcus, seeing that stars were truly reflected in her eyes, wanted desperately to kiss her, she gave him the perfect excuse.

'I've never known anybody like you, Marcus.'

And gently, and tentatively, he took it.


Having seen the lights switched off, heard the goodnights being called, and hearing Geoff drive away, Tessa, Kelly and PJ made their move. As PJ had promised, they had no problem getting into the games room window, but as they moved through the shadows towards the general room a voice crying out screechingly in the darkness froze them in their tracks. The voice came again.

'Good old Nelson!'

And PJ laughed.

'It's just Nicola's manky parrot!'

They crossed to look at it, and it stared back at them sourly, giving the odd inarticulate squawk.

They continued on their way, and PJ having sorted the lock out as Duncan had shown him, they were soon in the cellar. PJ headed confidently to the far corner, and Tessa and Kelly slightly less confidently followed on behind. 'This is very creepy!' Tessa decided without actually saying it. Then at one point Kelly screamed as a cobweb drifted over her face, scaring the life out of all of them. But they finally made the corner, and after some searching PJ found the trapdoor he was looking for in the floor. It was ancient and rusted, but they finally managed to swing it open, and they peered down into its musty darkness.

'Ugh! It smells!' Kelly said.

PJ dismissed it as a nothing.

'Just damp that's all. Right, are we going in?'

And they looked at each other in the light from their torches. Now the moment had come they weren't quite so sure it was a good idea.

Danny had been adamant he wasn't going ice skating again, he'd had enough last time, and Chrissie really got up his nose.

A little while later, he wondered why, if she got up his nose so much, how come he was spending his evening thinking about her? And then just a little while later, he decided as she had wanted him to go, she was probably thinking about him as well, so, deciding to do her a favour, he changed his mind and went.

Having hired skates and gone in, he soon wished he hadn't. Not only wasn't she thinking about him, but she was dancing with a sickeningly hunky young man who skated like a dream. And then he realised that he'd seen her skating with the same man the last time he was there as well, but then it didn't matter. Now, for some unknown reason, it did.

Danny decided to leave before she saw him, but before he could make his escape, Speedy spotted him, and came to drag him onto the ice, and for the second time running, Danny had a truly miserable night out ice skating.

Dropping down from the trapdoor the couple of metres into the sub-basement below, Tessa, Kelly and PJ found themselves in a small cave-like room. Their torches cutting through the blackness showed a low tunnel leading off in one corner. They went over there and all shone their torches along it. PJ peered in, but he couldn't see much as it quickly curved off to the right. It was Tessa who asked the question in a hushed voice.

'What is it? What can you see?'

PJ straightened up again.

'Not much, the roof's too low and it curves away. Kelly – you go first, you're the smallest.'

She tried to hide her fear.

'I hope there's not rats.'

PJ replied scathingly, 'I thought you were a country girl.'

Kelly replied as she ducked down low enough to get in, and headed off into the darkness at a crouch.

'That doesn't mean I can't be frightened.'

And with that as she stepped over an old pit prop lying in her path, and turned the corner, she screamed long and hard, and to Tessa and PJ's horror, the scream quickly faded away as if she was falling.

PJ reacted without thinking. He said,

'Wait here!' to Tessa, then he ducked down and went into the tunnel shouting as he did so.

'Hang on, Kelly! I'm coming!'

Rounding the corner he called back to Tessa:

'There's a hole here! I'm moving to the other side so I don't go down . . . !'

Then, absolutely horrified, Tessa heard PJ scream as well, and his scream too, was disappearing the way that Kelly's had. She shouted loudly.

'Kelly? PJ?'

And waited. Nothing. The second time she almost screamed it.

'Kelly!? PJ!?'

But only silence answered her.

They had both disappeared, and she was now totally alone.

# CHAPTER SIX

Debbie was walking home from skating with Nicola, feeling exhilarated.

'That was great, but I'll be stiff as a board tomorrow.'

It really had been a wonderful evening, Debbie decided. In fact if it wasn't for the niggling worry as to where Jemma had ran off to, it would have been perfect. She decided to get it off her chest.

'I hope Jemma's got home okay.'

But Nicola was in too good a mood to be over-fussed.

'Debs, stop worrying. You'll be grey before you're twenty-one.'

But then she stopped speaking as they turned the corner and the Grove came into view.

'What's that?'

But the question required no answer, for it was obvious Byker Grove was awash with fire engines, police cars, ambulances, and with what seemed like hundreds of people scurrying around in the light of searchlights that had been set up. They both knew something very bad had happened, and chances were it could involve Jemma.

Even though it was obvious Debbie still said it.

'It's the Grove! Come on!'

She was all ready to dash in that direction but Nicola, who was equally worried about Jemma, let commonsense prevail.

'We'd better get Dad!'

And they dashed to their house to tell him.

In the darkness of the sub-basement, at first Tessa had been too stunned to move, but finally she had gone carefully into the low tunnel following in their tracks.

She shone her torch around the corner and saw the hole in the floor of the narrow tunnel. She went to it carefully, and called down:

'Kelly? PJ?'

It was Kelly's voice that came back plaintively from the depths.

'My leg hurts.'

She didn't sound too far away. So Tessa put her hand into the hole hoping to pull her out.

'Can you reach my hand?'

Kelly tried and failed.

'I can't.

Tessa suddenly realised there was only one voice. 'Is PJ hurt?'

Kelly was slightly bemused.

'He isn't here.'

'He must be. He fell down with you.'

'He's not. There's nobody here...'

Tessa again shone her torch along the narrow tunnel, and saw there was another hole in the floor only a metre from the first. She went there and called, 'PJ!' but there was no reply. Shining her torch down, she saw that the hole, which was circular and only about half a metre in diameter, went down and down endlessly and her heart sank. If he had fallen down there he was in deep trouble. She went back and called to Kelly once more.

'I'll go and get help...'

But Kelly's voice was frightened and plaintive.

'Don't leave me ... Tessa, don't leave me on my own!'

Tessa hated doing it, but knew she had to get help.

'I won't be long, Kelly. But I've got to get somebody. Does your torch still work?'

Kelly called back.

'I don't know. It's down here somewhere.'

Tessa heard her searching for it, then light beamed upwards at her.

'Got it. It seems all right.'

'Good. Keep it on, and sing.'

Kelly was bemused. 'Sing?'

Tessa knew that was a good way to keep your spirits up.

'Yes. Hymns, pop songs, nursery rhymes, anything. Just keep on singing.' Tessa demonstrated, singing it loudly.

'All things bright and beautiful, all creatures great and small...'

And as Kelly started to join in, '... all things wise and wonderful, the Lord God made them all...' Tessa made her way back to the sub-basement, then climbed out to call the police.

When Nicola and Debbie broke the news to Alan he was on his feet in a flash, calling for Kath to ring Geoff, and then dashed for the Grove with Nicola and Debbie in close pursuit. Alan was amazed at the number of people who were milling round. It was obvious something major was afoot. A policeman stood guard at the door and wouldn't let him through.

'Sorry, sir, can't let you in.'

Alan explained the situation breathlessly.

'I live over there, my daughters are all members here. Is there a fire?'

The PC shook his head.

'Boy and girl trapped down in the foundations, far as we can make out.'

Nicola's heart skipped a beat as she heard him say it. She just had to know.

'What boy and girl?'

But he shook his head.

'Don't know yet, miss.'

Debbie, who had been trying to peer in the window, came back to Nicola's side, saw her face and knew something was very wrong.

'Nic? What is it?'

'There's two kids trapped under the cellar. Boy and a girl.'

'You think it could be Jemma? If that lunatic's made her go down there...!'

Nicola shook her head.

'We don't know it's Jem, Debs. It could be anybody.'

But Debbie wasn't to be consoled. She ran to the door screaming.

'Jemma! Jemma!'

But the policeman restrained her and stopped her getting past.

In the tunnel beyond the sub-basement Tessa, who had gone straight back down, having called the emergency services, left the Grove front doors wide open and all the lights blazing, comforted Kelly who was now softly crying, but soon she heard the fire engine and police sirens overhead.

'They're coming, Kelly! You're going to be all right! Kell?'

But Kelly wasn't to be placated.

'My torch has gone out and it's so dark down here. I'm scared.'

Tessa tried passing her hers but Kelly couldn't reach it, and she was afraid to drop it down the hole in case it broke and they were both left without light. So instead, she got Kelly talking about the old days, and the adventures they'd had in the past, to take her mind off it.

Having received Kath's call, Geoff had driven to the Grove at a speed that broke every rule in the book. Arriving with a screech of brakes, he leapt out and crossed to Alan.

'What is it, what's happened?'

Alan didn't waste words.

'Somebody's trapped in the cellars.'

'A burglar?'

'No, seems it's two of your kids.'

Debbie had come to listen.

'Only we don't know who.'

Tessa was relieved when the two burly fire-fighters finally arrived in the tunnel with powerful lights. She quickly explained what had happened, and when she mentioned the disappearance of PJ one of them crossed to shine his torch down the second narrow shaft, and then she saw him look to the other fireman in a way that made her heart drop. He didn't think there was much chance of PJ coming out alive.

Tessa had to move back to the small sub-basement room,

where more fire-fighters had arrived, so they could work in the tunnel, but when one of them said:

'You go back up into the house now, pet. One of the lads here'll take you.'

She had no hesitation.

'I'm staying till you've got her out.'

The one she'd spoken to leant down and called along the tunnel. 'How's she doing there? Do we need a stretcher?' and to Tessa's relief, the voice came echoing back.

'Bit shaken up, that's all. I don't think there's any serious harm. Stand by, we're bringing her up.'

And soon the firemen arrived in the sub-basement with a bedraggled and mud-spattered Kelly, her glasses broken but still perched on her nose. Tessa, seeing her safe, couldn't help but burst into tears, and flinging their arms around each other they both had a good comforting cry.


Geoff was talking to the fire Chief who was keeping in touch with the basement by radio, when the message came through that the girls, named Tessa and Kelly, were safe.

Debbie and Nicola standing nearby couldn't help but feel a great surge of relief. But what they heard next killed their joy stone dead. The Chief was explaining the situation to Geoff.

'Looks like it was an old mine shaft they fell into. There's still no sign of the boy, mind.'

Geoff said it quietly.

'What boy?'

'According to the girls, there was a lad with them.'

He then said the name as a question, as though he might have got it wrong.

'PJ?'

Geoff shook his head.

'That doesn't surprise me. So where is he?'

'That's just it. The girl who called us said he fell down another shaft. Only he's disappeared.'

Geoff was shocked.

'He's what?'

'Disappeared. We've got a couple of our lads trying to get

down there now, but I've got to be honest, it's a very deep shaft, and it doesn't look good.'

When PJ had gone into the narrow low tunnel after Kelly had screamed, he saw straight away that she'd gone down a hole. He guessed she probably hadn't seen it because it had over the years been covered by bits of straw and rubble. He'd then carefully stepped over that hole, not realising for one minute he could face exactly the same problem of hidden openings. It was only as the floor gave way beneath his feet, that he thought of it, and by then it was too late. He screamed without meaning to as he shot straight down like a plummeting stone. The thought that struck him on his way down was bizarre – he remembered Alice in *Alice in Wonderland* tumbling endlessly down the rabbit hole; but soon a more sinister thought struck. If he landed on concrete or stone at this speed he would break every bone in his body. But after what seemed forever, the tunnel started to slope instead of going straight down, and instead of plummeting he was sliding. He turned so his backside was taking the brunt rather than his stomach, and though it was agony he knew he was slowing down. Then the tunnel was gone and he was free falling, and two metres later, he was landing in a heap on a stone floor.

He stood and tentatively checked to see if he had broken anything. Nothing was. He then realised he had been hanging on to the torch like grim death, and by a miracle, when he switched it on, it had still worked. Its light showed he was in an old mine shaft. The tunnel he had come down was obviously a vent hole for breathing, but why it should end in Byker sub-basement he couldn't imagine. One thing was sure, there was no way he could get out that way again. So he set off walking, looking for an exit.

He walked for what seemed like hours up and down what turned out to be a warren of passageways, and had almost given up hope when he felt a breeze blowing in the distance. Realising that where there was breezes there was quite often openings, he followed it, and finally pushing through some overgrown weeds, he was back in the open air once more. He thought he'd walked so far he must have been in the centre of Newcastle, so was amazed when he looked around to see that he was in a grove of trees less than a couple of hundred metres from the front door. Not only that, but among all the gathered vehicles with their flashing lights, he could see Geoff chatting to a fireman. He set off in that direction.

He reached them just as Geoff was saying, 'What's the chance of finding him?' And the fireman answering glumly. 'We'll find him all right, but whether we'll find him alive . . .'

Geoff shook his head sadly.

'Poor old PJ.'

And PJ nonchalantly replied, 'Naw! It's all right, Geoff, man. Just a bit bruised that's all.'

And as Geoff jumped with the shock of it, Tessa came out of the front door, saw that PJ was standing there safe, and ran to cuddle him with relief.


When Nicola and Debbie finally got home, they found that Jemma was safely tucked up in bed, where she had been all evening since leaving the skating rink.

The next morning Debbie and Nicola had a post-mortem on the last evening's events, but as Tessa had been too upset to talk about it, it was going to require further investigation later. Alan's arrival stopped the discussion. They greeted him, with Nicola adding,

'How's Mam?'

Alan went on sorting the post as he spoke.

'Still a bit queasy. One for you, Nicola.'

As he passed it to her, Debbie said,

'Who's it from?'

To which he replied, 'I don't know, nosy, but it looks official.'

Nicola quickly ripped it open, and gave her the answer.

'It's from the social services. They want me and Charlie to go and see them.'

Debbie was perplexed.

'What for?'

Nicola shook her head.

'It must be about Doyle. Perhaps they want to tell us off.'

But Alan wasn't having that.

'Don't be ridiculous, pet. Why would they?'

Nicola looked at him.

'We told them we were taking on a responsibility, and we let them down.'

Debbie didn't mince words.

'That's rubbish.'

Alan agreed.

'Debbie's right.' He glanced at the clock. 'Right – I'd best be off. One of you'll take your mam up a cup of tea, won't you? And perhaps a bit of toast.'

Jemma entered the room looking a bit down, heard the request and made the offer.

'I'll do it.'

Pleased, Alan said his goodbyes and went. Nicola looked at Jemma as she slumped into her chair at the table.

'So, what happened to you last night? You flashed out of the ice rink like a Scud missile.'

'Nothing happened,' Jemma said glumly.

Debbie checked it tentatively.

'You mean you just came home? You didn't see Lee?'

Jemma nodded.

'Couldn't find him, could I?' Then she looked at both of them.

'I only wanted us all to be friends. What's so terrible in that?'

Nicola saw that Jemma meant it.

'Nothing, Jem. But sometimes things just don't work out, no matter how hard you want them to.'

Jemma shook her head in disbelief.

'You've got Lee all wrong. You've all took against him and it's not fair.'

Debbie remained calm, she didn't want Jemma to get in a screaming rage again, as she had been doing whenever Lee's name was mentioned recently.

'He's done a lot of awful stuff, Jemma. We're not making that up.'

Jemma answered plaintively, just wishing they could understand.

'But he's explained it to us.'

Debbie gave her the chance to tell them.

'Go on, then.'

But Jemma had given her word.

'I promised not to tell.'

Nicola said it quietly and coolly.

'Thing is – do you believe him, Jemma?'

And for the first time Jemma sat back and really thought about it. Did she?

And Debbie decided that after Nicola had gone, she would try to get the inside story out of Jemma.

At the Grove, Tessa sat and faced a very serious Geoff who had asked her to come in early. She finally broke the silence that had fallen between them after the 'Hellos' had been exchanged.

'I suppose I'm in trouble?'

'I shan't be pinning any medals on you, miss, that's for sure. What did Mr and Mrs Skerratt have to say?'

Tessa thought about the people she was staying with. They were nice, she didn't like causing them heartache, and she knew in this case she had.

'They decided not to tell my parents, but they gave me a good old rollocking.'

Geoff nodded agreeably.

'I'll bet they did.'

And then he got it underway.

'What on earth were you thinking of, Tessa – I always regarded you as one of our more level headed members?'

Tessa thought about it.

'I just got carried away, I guess.'

'Did it not occur to you to ask me first?'

And Tessa gave the obvious reply.

'I knew you wouldn't let us.'

Geoff had to agree with that.

'Too right I wouldn't. You do realise the lot of you could have broken your necks down there?'

Tessa was quick to point out the truth of the matter.

'It's not PJ or Kelly's fault, it was all my idea. I wanted to find the priest hole so much I didn't stop to think it might be dangerous.'

She added her final thought with sincerity.

'I'm sorry. I truly am.'

And Geoff seeing she meant it decided to take no further action.

'Yes, well, I should think so. You should just be thankful they're both all right.'

And Tessa told him her secret.

'I prayed for them. I've never prayed so hard for anything as I did last night.'

Geoff said it with sincerity.

'Thank God your prayers were answered.'

Even though he was still a bit bruised and had earned himself the day off, PJ managed to be at the school gates when it came out, and soon was the centre of attention, telling his tale of plunging down mine shafts, and wandering in the bowels of Newcastle, to wide-eyed juniors. But then, seeing Lee in the distance, he remembered a promise he'd made to Debbie earlier in the day, so he said his goodbyes, and set off after him.

Jemma had finally told Debbie the truth about Lee's situation at home, and before school Debbie had rung PJ both to see if he was all right after his adventure, and to let him know they may have got Lee wrong.

PJ had decided there was only one way to find out, a bit of detective work, and that was what he was now intent on doing.

Nicola had passed on the message from the social services to Charlie, and straight after school they both went round there feeling a bit timorous. They were in the office for less than five minutes, and when they were back out on the pavement with Nicola holding the large brown envelope they'd been given, they stared at each other in total disbelief.

'I don't believe it. Why would he do a thing like that? Why us?'

Charlie just repeated what they'd been told.

'As the social worker said – because there was nobody else.'

Nicola said it sadly.

'He only had just you and me. And we let him down.'

'Don't start that again. You'll only make it worse.'

But Nicola was on a downer.

'It couldn't be worse, could it? I couldn't feel worse if I tried.'

Charlie tried to jolly her out of it.

'It's not that tragic, Nic. Come on! We can have a great time!'

The thought suddenly struck Nicola and she looked at Charlie intently.

'There is one thing we can do to help put things right ...'

And with Nicola in this mood, Charlie dreaded to think what that might be, and thought to herself, 'Being left all Doyle's worldly possessions, plus five hundred pounds, might still turn out to be not a lot of fun.'

PJ quite enjoyed tailing Lee while keeping out of sight. He decided that if things were a bit quiet on the job front when he finally left school he might set up a detective agency. Later, after he'd been sat on a wall a little distance from the house Lee had gone into, for nearly an hour while waiting for him to leave again, PJ wasn't quite so sure about it. This detective business could get boring.

But finally he was relieved to see Lee leave the house, and as soon as he was out of sight PJ crossed the street and rang the doorbell.

And within five minutes, he knew the truth of the matter.

In the Grove general room, Winston was intent on giving Tessa a dressing down for putting his friend Kelly at risk, and leaving her bruised and housebound until further notice.

'You were a right plonker, dragging her down there, Tessa!'

But Tessa gave as good as she got.

'Don't get stroppy with me, Rambo. I didn't "drag" her down there, she volunteered.'

The parrot in the corner threw in its comment.

'Silly old fool, silly old fool.'

And Tessa shouted back at it:

'Oh, shut up, you talking feather duster!'

Angel, who was sitting with Noddy, had been all ears as Tessa and Winston argued, and was now all eyes as she asked the question.

'What was it like, anyroad? Were there skeletons?'

Debbie threw in the thought before Tessa had chance to answer.

'Weren't you scared? Must have been dead creepy. Ugh.'

Noddy was quite perky about it.

'You should have asked us. I like anything like that, me.'

Angel didn't believe him.

'You don't!'

'I do. I slept the night in a crypt once.'

With that, all eyes were on him. He finally confessed.

'Well, it's more a caravan site now, but the man said where me dad parked our van used to be a crypt.'

Tessa said her inner thought out loud.

'I'll never know if there was priest hole there now.'

Speedy passing by spelt it out.

'Dead right, you won't. Geoff'd never let nobody down there again in a million years.'

Debbie added, 'Besides, we're moving out any day, remember?'

And at that thought glumness fell over all of them like a pall.

Spuggie walked straight into the pall with a bright beaming smile on her face.

'Hiya! Isn't it a fantastic day! Is Marcus here yet?'

And then seeing the looks on the faces around, said, 'What's the matter?'

But nobody had the heart to tell her.


Danny bumped into Chrissie at the gates, and walked up the drive with her. The silence held until she chuckled gently. Danny asked what it was.

Chrissie replied with a smile. 'I just remembered that day on the tow path. I thought you were a right twit, charging up brandishing your milk bottle.'

Danny decided not to take umbrage.

'Twit? Don't forget I could have saved your life!'

But Chrissie wasn't having that.

'That pimply wimp wasn't a threat.' Then she remembered. 'Still, I don't think I ever said thanks.'

Danny agreed.

'I don't think you did.'

Chrissie went on.

'Won't need rescuing in future now, will I? Not after Lloyd's done his stuff.'

Danny decided to check out if the fellow he'd seen her with was her boyfriend or not. What better way than to offer a date.

'There's a Kung Fu movie on tonight, fancy coming?'

Chrissie shook her head.

'Sorry, I've got skating practice.'

'Can't you skip it?'

She was adamant.

'No, I can't skip it, it's important. You're as bad as me mam, mithering me to babysit tonight.'

'Why tonight?'

'It's their anniversary.'

'Wedding?'

Chrissie nodded.

'Twenty-fifth. I told her, if I'm going to be a professional I've got to stick at it.'

Danny was appalled at her self-centredness.

'But that was for something special.'

She was surprised at his heated reaction.

'So's this. My future.'

Danny shook his head in disbelief.

'You could have given up one rotten night.'

Now she was quietly furious.

'What's it to do with you, anyway?'

'I don't understand you.'

'Because I know what I want? Because I've got a goal in life?'

Danny coldly spelt it out.

'I'd call it just plain selfish.'

And she hit the roof.

'Did I ask you? Did I?'

And with that she was storming off up the path. Danny called after her as she went.

'And you never did says thanks!'

As he watched her walk away, a van passed and then came to a halt a little way up the drive. Danny watched as the three men inside got out and started taking surveyor's equipment from the back, then Danny realised the first stages of building work were obviously underway.

At the Day Centre, Charlie and Nicola were the focus of everybody's attention, with Alan Dobson standing close by, as the lady who organised the Centre made her little speech.

'You all know about the sad passing away of poor Mr Doyle; well, apparently he bequeathed all his worldly goods to these two young ladies, who were so kind to him at the end of his life.'

Nicola thought, 'If only they knew.'

'And they have very generously given us the TV set he left them, to replace our old one.' Alan, who had brought it in his van, whispered to them.

'It's a little beauty, is this. Are you sure you want to give it away?'

Nicola nodded.

'Yes, Dad. We're quite sure.'

Charlie could only shrug, thinking to herself, 'Bang goes a nice telly.'

All the Grove girls were in serious discussion with Alison re. the possibility of having a 'ladies only' room at whatever place they finally ended up in. Angel spelt it out.

'We want a place where we can talk about things we don't want them to hear,' she pointed at the few lads scattered around, ''cos they laugh.'

Spuggie leapt to the defence of her own particular favourite male.

'Marcus doesn't.'

And Debbie to hers.

'PJ doesn't either.'

Alison thought a ladies room wasn't a bad idea.

'I'll do my best. Even if we have to build a little shed outside.'

Chrissie, seeing Danny enter and cross to where Geoff was standing near the tea bar, said it acidly.

'We certainly need somewhere we can get away from those wallies.'

Reaching Geoff, Danny said it quite quietly.

'Geoff, I think you'd better come outside.'

But most managed to hear, and all followed Geoff through the doors and outside onto the porch.

The men in the Grove grounds had set up their equipment and were busily taking soundings from the ground.

It was Spuggie who asked the question for all of them.

'What are they doing?'

Geoff had no idea but took a stab at it anyway.

'Making sure there's no unexploded bombs when they knock us down, I expect.'

Speedy's comment was heartfelt.

'I wish there was.'


Jemma was heading for the Grove, wishing she was likely to see Lee there, but knowing that she wasn't. She heard someone call her, turned to look, and saw it was PJ chasing up the path after her. He spoke as soon as he reached her.

'I've just seen your friend Lee.'

Jemma guessed there was more to come.

'Oh yes?'

PJ didn't want to give away the fact he already knew the answer to the question, so decided he must drag it out of her somehow.

'What did he tell you about why he went begging? Come on, he must have told you some tale.'

But he didn't have to battle for an answer.

Jemma decided to shame him.

'It's a secret; but if you must know it's to help his dad. The betting on the cycle race was the same. His mam's dead and they've got three little kids besides him, so there! Proud of yourself?'

PJ shook his head sadly. He knew what he was going to say would hurt.

'There's just the one little brother, Jemma. He's five.'

Jemma answered defiantly.

'So? They've still got no mam and his dad's out of work and . . .'

PJ shook his head again, interrupting as he did so.

'. . . His dad's not out of work, and they live in a nice house, they're not poor at all.'

Jemma asked it icily.

'How do you know all this?'

PJ decided to tell her the truth.

'Because I followed him home.'

Jemma was outraged.

'That's a disgusting, sneaky thing to do!'

But PJ wouldn't accept that undefended.

'Not half as disgusting as telling you a load of old lies.' And then he pressed his point home. 'His mam's not dead, Jemma. I spoke to her. She's the one who told me. Now do you believe us when we say he's no good?'

Jemma simply stared at him wide-eyed with disbelief, then turned and ran down the path back to the gates.

In the Metro Centre, Charlie saw the most beautiful dress ever, in *Frock Shop*.

She pointed it out to Nicola.

'I can just see myself in that!'

And then looking round the window she saw one that was perfect for Nicola as well.

'And that'd look brilliant on you! Come on, let's try 'em on.'

But Nicola was still intent on spending their big day playing the responsible lady.

'Charlie, how many more times, we can't spend that money on ourselves!'

And Charlie had nearly had enough of it.

'Why not? He left it to us, didn't he?'

Nicola spelt it out.

'On condition we look after Nelson.'

'So we'll look after Nelson, it doesn't take five hundred quid to feed one mangy old parrot even if he lives to be a hundred!'

But Nicola wasn't to be sidetracked so easily.

'It's Doyle's life savings. It'd not be right to blow it on a stupid spending spree.'

Charlie, at the end of her tether, finally blew.

'Honestly, you make me sick sometimes, Nicola Dobson! Always such a blimmin' Goody Goody. Well you can put your half in the collecting box for lame ducks if you want, but I'm not.'

Nicola was appalled.

'You sound just like Donna.'

'At least Donna knew how to have fun!'

And with that Charlie stormed into the shop, dead set on at least trying on the dress.

It looked awful on her.

Jemma caught up with Lee near the underpass. He was in his begging clothes and heading for the stairs. As he saw her he smiled, and came across to her.

'Hi. Sorry about me vanishing act last night, just did my brains in when I saw you with that bunch of goons.'

Jemma said it calmly, viewing what he was wearing.

'I thought you might still be doing this.'

Lee sniffed disdainfully.

'You don't think I take any notice of that Geoff Keegan, do you?' He looked at the crowd scurrying past. 'Good dosh just now, all the typists coming home from work.'

He put on his whiney beggar-boy voice.

'Please, lady, I've not had 'owt to eat since yesterday.'

Jemma shook her head in sheer disbelief.

'You don't give a button for nobody, do you?'

Lee looked at her, surprised.

'Why should I?'

Jemma let him have it full blast.

'That why you fed us all that guff about your poor old dad; and having no mam; and poor little starving kid brothers and sisters, Jack and Jill and Tom Thumb. Fairy tales all of it?'

Lee smiled at the thought.

'Yeah. Neat touch that, I thought. Little Tom Thumb.'

Jemma had set out to be furious, but was by now totally impressed by his sheer nerve, she'd never met anyone like him.

'You admit it was all lies, then?'

Lee shrugged.

'Sure. More interesting than the truth any time. The truth's dead boring.'

Then there was a touch of surprise in his voice.

'Are you mad at me?'

And Jemma realised that she wasn't any more; so didn't come across at all convincingly when she lied.

'Course I am. Taking us for a fool.'

And seeing that she was lying, and wasn't very good at it, Lee smiled again. Then she finally smiled as well, and linking arms with him she said, 'Come on, then. Show us how you do it.'

And they went down into the subway together, and Jemma was never going to be the same sweet little girl again.


In the Grove there was a major mystery afoot. The case of the missing parrot; or more to the point – who left Nelson's door open and thereby allowed him to fly out and escape. The whole building was searched from top to bottom, everybody joining in the search except Charlie, who was deep in conversation with Speedy in the games room.

Nicola went there to face her, and arrived as Charlie was saying, 'So you're on, then?'

And Speedy, his face wreathed in smiles, answered, 'Yeah, I'm game. Sounds brilliant!'

Nicola butted in swinging Charlie round to face her.

'You did it on purpose, didn't you? You let Nelson out!'

'I don't know what you're talking about.'

Nicola yelled it.

'You thought with him gone you could spend the money on what you want.'

Charlie matched her yell for yell.

'I can anyway. You're off your trolley.'

And with that Nicola turned and stormed out.

Speedy had simply watched the brief battle bemused. But Charlie hadn't even lost her place in the conversation, and simply carried on as though nothing had happened.

'Right, then. Here's the plan...'

Speedy couldn't believe his luck, Charlie was taking him out for a day in London. Could this possibly mean ... but he didn't even dare think it.

While Speedy had no trouble getting up at the crack of dawn on the following Saturday, the day of his and Charlie's journey to the big city, Danny was thinking it may well be time to call it a day on the milk round.

He was shattered, and delivered the bottles on automatic pilot. As was the usual way on a Saturday morning, he collected money from any one who was up and about, putting the money in the leather pouch tied at his waist.

About halfway through his round, Danny woke up with a vengeance when two yobs, appearing from nowhere, grabbed him and tried to get the pouch off him. He shouted at the top of his voice.

'Get off! Let go!'

The biggest youth said it threateningly.

'Come on, hand it over, if you don't want us to spoil that pretty face of yours.'

But Danny was adamant.

'No way!'

Lloyd had only shown the Tai Chi class two things; a neck lock, and a kick.

Danny used the kick on the big guy, and was thrilled to see him immediately doubling up. He used the neck lock on the other, and in seconds it was over as the man begged for mercy. Danny let him go, and they both went running for it. Danny watched them go with satisfaction, and couldn't wait to get to the Grove to spread the word on how brilliant Tai Chi was for self-defence.

Lloyd was in the tea bar chatting to Alison, when Noddy passing through made the comment.

'It's a good thing you're teaching us this Tai Chi stuff, Lloyd. Danny's just given some lads what for with it.'

But Lloyd saying 'He's what?' and heading for the general room, made Noddy think that maybe he'd got it wrong, so he followed to see what was said.

As Lloyd arrived Danny was telling his story yet again.

'... and the guy in the neck lock was begging for mercy...'

Lloyd's voice cut through the story imperiously.

'Right! What's all this about?'

And it was Chrissie who told it.

'Danny's just showing us how he played the big hero.'

Angel chipped in.

'He was attacked by these yobs who tried to pinch his milk money.'

Danny smiled.

'Don't worry, Lloyd, I saw them both off.'

Lloyd's face was red with anger, but he managed to contain it – just.

He spoke loudly enough for the whole room to hear.

'I want you all to listen to this, not just Danny.'

But it was to Danny he directed it.

'What you did was stupid.'

Danny was shocked. 'What?'

Lloyd spelt it out.

'You're like a kid running around with a loaded gun. You don't know how dangerous it can be, to yourself as well as the other guy.'

But now Winston butted in.

'How can it be dangerous? You are teaching us self-defence, man.'

'Teaching is the operative word. I've only just started. You've all got to learn, and until you've learnt you don't put *anything* I've shown you into operation. And you certainly don't go getting cocky about it.'

Danny was really choked. Shown up in front of everyone and put down. He asked the question with a sulky and sarcastic edge.

'So what should I have done then? Let them get away with the cash?'

There was no hesitation.

'If that's what it took – yes. Better than one of you winding up with a broken neck.'

The silence held as Lloyd looked from face to face. Finally he said it.

'If you're still as keen on learning to do it right, how about an extra class later this afternoon?'

And all except Danny agreed enthusiastically. Lloyd realised it would take Danny a while to recover from the public put-down, but what he'd told them, needed to be told.


A little while later PJ broke the news to Debbie, about his conversation with Jemma, confirming Lee was a lying con man.

'And you told her it was all lies?'

'Every word.'

And then he gave his opinion.

'I still think it may not make any difference, Debbie.'

She shook her head, completely at a loss.

'PJ, what are we going to do?'

He thought about it.

'Not much more you can do now. Young Jemma's just going to have to learn the hard way.'

At that Nicola walked in and saw the parrot cage was still empty, and even though it was obvious, still asked anyway.

'Nelson not turned up then?'

PJ and Debbie shook their heads.

Nicola slumped in a chair, shattered.

'I've been everywhere. I even went to Doyle's old house but there's no sign of him.'

She looked around the room.

'Where's Charlie? I suppose it's too much to expect she'll be out looking for him?'

It was Spuggie who threw it in from where she sat reading in the corner.

'Not unless it's gone to London. 'Cos that's where she's gone with Speedy.'

Nicola was amazed.

'London?'

Spuggie nodded.

'They got the first train. Speedy was dead excited. Lucky pig. Wish I could get somebody to buy me a ticket to America.'

Speedy decided he had had quite simply the best day of his life. And it had been all expenses paid, with the most beautiful woman in the world, Charlie.

They had seen everything it was possible for a tourist to see in London in one brief day, but coming back on the train that evening, Speedy thought it really didn't matter, as he was going to go back there again and again. Now he was just desperate to get to the Grove so he could have a good brag about it.

Charlie looked at him sitting opposite her on the speeding train and said it quietly.

'Enjoy it?'

He nodded happily.

'Best day ever, Charlie. Best day ever.'

His joy didn't last long. When they finally arrived at the Grove, which was packed with all the gang and full of laughter and chat, Nicola exploded as they walked through the door, screaming at Charlie:

'You spent it, didn't you! You blew all of Doyle's money on a stupid day out!'

And silence immediately fell in the room as Charlie faced her. She said it calmly.

'As a matter of fact I haven't spent it all, but I've had a fantastic time and don't regret it one bit.'

Nicola's fury was unabated.

'I'll bet you don't. That's all you think about, yourself, you're just rotten selfish.'

Speedy was about to leap to Charlie's defence when Charlie got it in first.

'Speedy said he's had the best day of his whole life, and he's not had much of a life. If you call that being selfish, well okay, I'm selfish.'

Nicola was a bit thrown at that, but still thought she had a point, and pressed it home.

'All the same you'd no right to have just gone off and done it without telling me. Doyle left that money between us.'

Finally Charlie had had enough.

'Doyle, Doyle, Doyle! That's all I ever hear!'

She stuck her hand in her pocket and brought out what was left of the money, rolled in tight wad and fastened with an elastic band.

'Here's the rest of the money, do what you want with it.'

With that she threw it at Nicola hard. It hit her and bounced off to lie on the floor at her feet. Charlie looked round the gathered crowd momentarily, then turned and stormed out.

The conversations were instantly underway again as all the kids talked about the row, and as Nicola bent and picked the roll of money off the floor.

Speedy crossed to her saying, 'I'm sorry. I didn't know about the money.' And then he added, heartfelt, 'But it was a grand day out.'

Nicola was looking thoughtful as she spoke.

'That's all right, Speedy. It wasn't your fault.'

Spuggie saw the door open and saw that it was Amanda and Marcus arriving. She called to Marcus.

'Hiya! Did you see Venus?'

'No. it was too cloudy.'

And then to Spuggie's amazement, Marcus called for quiet in a loud voice.

Slowly the noise tailed away.

Geoff, who had been talking to Alan in the tea bar, came through the general room to see what was going on, and Alison also arrived from the office. The silence fell and held. Then Marcus spoke again.

'Amanda's got some news.'

But she shook her head.

'No. Marcus has.'

Then she nudged him to speak. And he did.

'It's about Prestige Properties.'

The silence was now total.

Marcus looked from face to face in the crowded room, and realised they were hanging onto his every word. Finally he let them have it:

'When they heard about Kelly and PJ falling down the mine shafts, they made a lot more enquiries. They've found out that the whole place is riddled with mine workings.'

Amanda joined in the telling.

'It seems the tunnel PJ fell into is just one of dozens.'

Tessa's eyes were gleaming.

'You mean there's loads of old tunnels down there?'

And Geoff calling, 'Don't even think it, Tessa!' set everybody laughing and broke the tension slightly. Geoff continued to speak, directing his question at Amanda and Marcus.

'So how does that effect things?'

Amanda said it, quietly thrilled.

'They're pulling out.'

There was a gasp of amazement from the gathered group. Marcus picked up the story again.

'The really good news is that Father ... Dad doesn't think anybody else will be interested either. Byker Grove is safe for ever.'

And the cheer that went up could be heard to the very gates of Byker, and the way everybody gathered round Amanda and Marcus slapping them on the back, and generally making them feel welcome and special, told them both, that finally they were to be accepted as part of the gang.

As the wild jollification continued, the front door opened and Kelly, still looking bruised and scratched, arrived helping herself with a pair of crutches. She couldn't manage to close the door behind, but simply hobbled forward into the room, and Tessa seeing her there dashed to her side screaming her name, and making everyone look in that direction.

'Kelly! What the heck are you doing here?'

Kelly said it a bit shamefaced.

'I made me dad bring me. I said I had to let Geoff see I'm

159

okay apart from a few scratches. I didn't want you getting into trouble.'

Geoff said it happily.

'Personally I think we should all be thanking Kelly.'

Kelly was amazed.

'I thought you might tell us off.'

Geoff nodded his head.

'I might well have done. But thanks to you falling down that hole, Prestige Properties have backed out of the deal. So I say three cheers for Kelly!'

As the cheers rang out loud and clear, and Kelly blushed scarlet, as if attracted by the noise, into the open front door walked a very manky parrot called Nelson, saying 'Silly old fool!' over and over again as he approached the general room, and the noisy throng within.


It was only a fortnight later that Spuggie's dream came true.

She stood in the airport lounge with Fraser as her flight to America was called over the tannoy, and she then headed with him for the entrance to the transit lounge.

At the last moment before going through, Spuggie gave him a hug.

He smiled at her, thrilled she was so obviously over the moon.

'Off you go, Spuggie – have a great time.'

She nodded. And then, for what he thought must be the hundredth time, she said,

'You won't forget to thank Nicola again?'

Fraser shook his head.

'I won't forget.'

And with that, having waved goodbye one last time, she went through the door into the transit lounge, and set out on the greatest adventure of her life.